ARROGANT ARRIVAL

GAIL HARIS

This book contains adult / mature situations.
Arrogant Arrival © 2020 by Gail Haris
and Gail Haris LLC
Copyright Cocky Hero Club, Inc.
All rights reserved.

The scanning, uploading, and electronic sharing of any part of this book without the author's permission is piracy and theft of the author's intellectual property. No part of this book may be reproduced or transmitted in any form without written permission by the author, except for the use of brief passage for review purposes only.

This book is a work of fiction. Names, businesses, places, and events are all used in fictitious manner or of the author's imagination. Any resemble to any person alive or dead, or any events or occurrences, is solely coincidental. The characters and story lines are created by the author's imagination and are used fictitiously.

Editor: Elaine York,
www.allusiongraphics.com
Formatting: Allusions Graphics,
www.allusiongraphics.com
Cover Design: Letitia Hasser,
www.rbadesigns.com

ARROGANT ARRIVAL

Arrogant Arrival is a standalone story inspired by Vi Keeland and Penelope Ward's *Mr. Moneybags* and *Playboy Pilot*. It's published as part of the Cocky Hero Club world, a series of original works, written by various authors, and inspired by Keeland and Ward's *New York Times* bestselling series. "

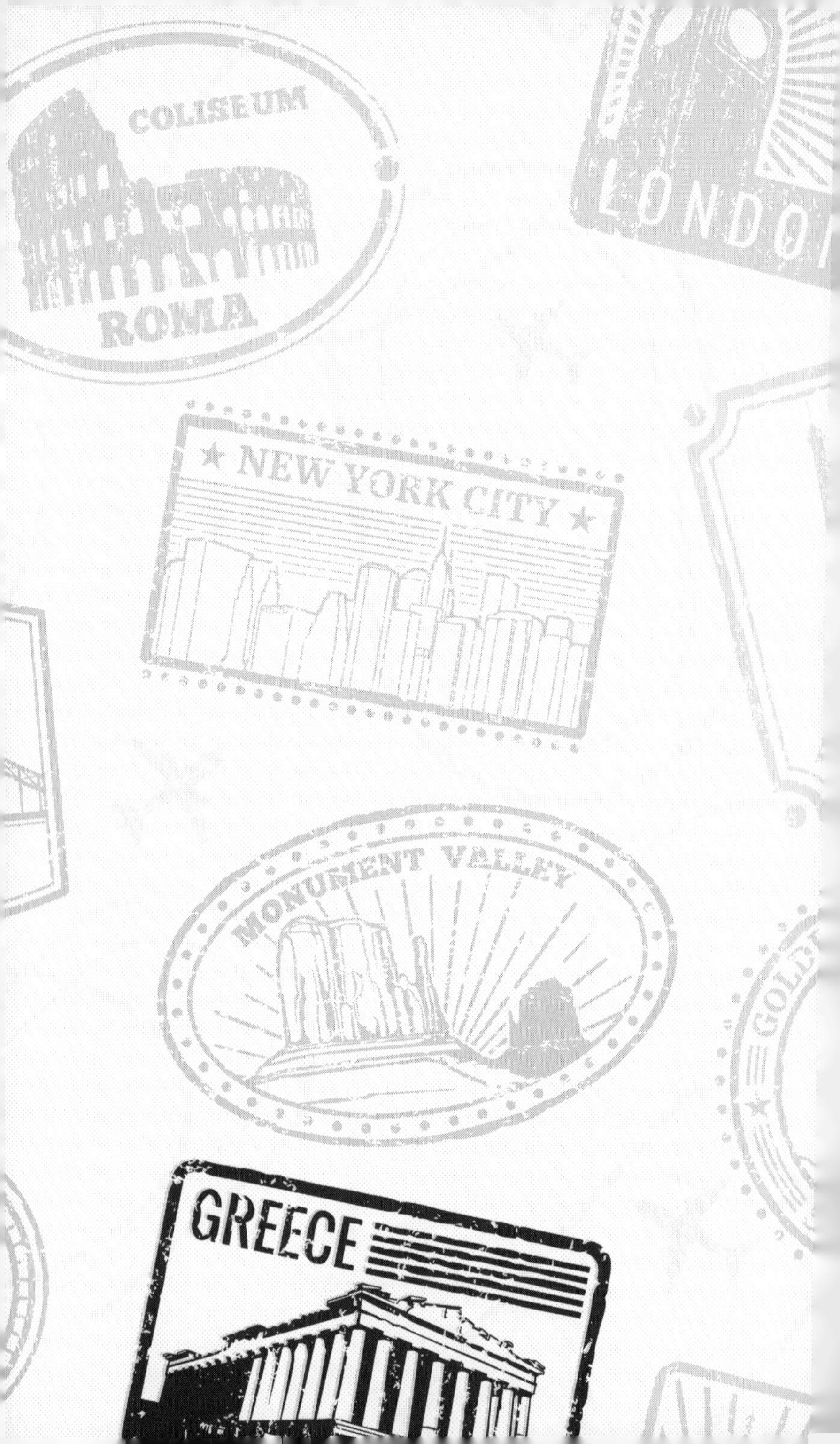
COLISEUM
ROMA
NEW YORK CITY
MONUMENT VALLEY
GREECE

CHAPTER 1

Jolene

Dear Journal,

I did it again. And again. And fucking again. When will I ever learn? I spent my layover in New York City. Bright lights, big city, and the pilots here are shitty. I fell for it again. At first, I was so excited to share a night out with Daniel. He's a native of the Big Apple and offered for me to stay at his place instead of one of the hotels the airline puts us in. He did take me to the most amazing hot dog stand on the corner of 5th and 37th. Quite frankly, that was the best wiener I got last night. Pun intended. Bigger and more satisfying. This morning we rode to the airport together, and he kept his hand on my lower back the entire time we walked to the terminal. However, his hand fell from my back so fast when he saw the new and younger woman waiting at the gate. With a *wink and a nod, Daniel walked away from me. He left me standing there to watch as he used the same charm on her that he'd used on me the past couple of flights. I thought I could handle it. My mask of false bravado remained firmly in place until our flight. I underestimated how fast he moves and how little I must've meant to him. He winked at me when I opened the door to the cockpit. That fucking wink again. I've finally come to terms with it. After years of denial and chasing after the idea that I could find romance in the sky, I've come to the conclusion that all pilots are the same: arrogant assholes.*

The ink smears as a tear drop lands on the paper. Shit. I can't believe I'm actually going to cry over that prick. I didn't even like him that much. Shoving my journal into my oversized purse, I stand and rush to the restroom so I can clean myself up before my next flight.

"Jolene! Wait up!" My two crew members and best friends rush over and follow me into the women's restroom.

"This is bullshit. They're all pigs." I grab a makeup remover wipe from my purse and dab away the smeared eyeliner from under my eyes.

"Dogs," Lana throws out.

"Rats," Renee adds.

I smile at the reflection of my two colleagues behind me. Their hands are on their hips, ready to tackle any problem I have. They've become my family in the sky. We could all three easily pass for sisters, and

ARROGANT ARRIVAL

passengers often ask us if we're triplets. All three of us are dressed in navy International Airlines' stewardess uniforms, black hair pulled up high in neat buns, and our makeup applied the same, neat and clean. Well... mine was the same until I started crying.

I brought this upon my foolish self. Three months spent being a glorified booty call for Captain Dickhead. *Okay, that wasn't really his name.* It is now as far as I'm concerned. He tossed me aside, pretending like there'd never been *anything* between us as soon as he met his new *co-pilot*. God, that was a terrible flight. I can't believe I opened the door to her assisting him with his *joystick*. The way he looked at me. There was no regret in his eyes at all. He just calmly told me to please close the door. Then, after the flight, he actually had the balls to say, *"You can't be serious? I didn't cheat on you. We'd have to be in a relationship for that to happen. We were having some fun. That's all there was between us. Two co-workers having fun and killing time on layovers."*

Then he walked off with *her,* his new favorite co-worker. This keeps happening to me. *Because I fall for it every time. Because I'm a fool.* But not anymore. "Thanks, girls. But I mean it. I'm done. I will *never, ever, ever* sleep with another pilot."

"We've all said that and meant it at one time or another." Lana sighs.

"Until the next long layover." Renee giggles. "I think it's that sexy-as-hell uniform and how well they fill it out that does it," she says thoughtfully. Lana nods in agreement.

"Well, there won't be another uniform next to mine on a hotel room floor anytime in the near future.

I've gotten my heart broken by a pilot too many times. They'll have to find something else to *lay* on their overnight trips." I toss the wipe in the trash, fluff my hair, and straighten my uniform.

"That's right!"

Lana turns her head to stare at Renee's enthusiasm. "Are you calling off pilots, too?"

"Oh, God, no. I prefer my uniform to be spread eagle next to theirs on that hotel room floor any given day of the week. I'm just being supportive. Each to their own, I say."

I try to smile but it comes off weak. I'm too aggravated with myself. I mean, it's not like I didn't do my fair share of seduction. It's just that I end up falling for them and that's the danger zone. Then I'd think after a month or two, I'd changed them. With my womanly wiles, I would be the one to tame him. But I was never that girl. I was never that special someone. Is it so wrong to want to be her? To be *the one* for someone? That's not asking a lot, is it?

We exit the women's restroom and dodge travelers moving quickly through JFK airport. We'd just gotten back to the US from an overseas flight, and now we are working a connecting flight to Miami. At first, life in the sky was exciting and I loved traveling to all the airport hub hops. But I'm not twenty-three anymore. Now at twenty-nine, I'm ready to have something more solid. I'd like to be a little more grounded, if you will. Pun totally intended.

Almost as if she can hear my thoughts, Lana places a hand on my shoulder and says, "Your Mr. Right will arrive, Jolene, I can feel it."

ARROGANT ARRIVAL

I place my hand on top of hers and give a gentle squeeze. "Thanks, Lana. I know he will. The only difference is that I know that his cock won't be from the cockpit of the plane."

Lana and Renee both burst out laughing.

"No, but you still might find him in the clouds. Maybe a handsome, lonely passenger who wants the same as you do. Both of you searching for the ultimate soulmate while soaring across the sky. Traveling the world in search of your one true love." Lana's eyes are bright with excitement.

I roll my eyes, "You need to get your own head out of the clouds."

Renee ignores my remark and nudges me. "Yeah, you might just find him in 16B"

We all three giggle. I shake my head, "As long as he isn't flying the plane. Now, let's all go see who's occupying 16B on our flight to Miami."

My chest tightens as I spot Captain Carter Clynes, or as we all call him, Trip, boarding the plane. I hate how my heart still skips a beat at the sight of him. He's another one of the pilots I, at one time, thought I could share *more* with. It's been two years since we had a *thing*. It only lasted two months, but that was a record for him. We weren't exclusive, and he had made that clear. We had a lot of fun, but my stupid heart had to start getting involved. I, for sure, thought he was going to fall for me as well, he just needed time. But then we had a layover and he entered the hotel with a *passenger*, Kendall

Sparks. Now they're married and she's pregnant. If he hadn't met her—could it have been me? Most likely not and I've accepted that fact. Besides, I'm honestly happy Trip found love. Kendall turned him into an even better man.

Lana's hand on my arm draws my attention away from the gorgeous captain. Her wide smile has me smiling before I even know what she's going to say.

"Did you see him?"

"See who?"

"16B!"

She's gotta be messing with me. 16B is probably some eighty-five-year-old man wearing flip flops and socks like the typical tourists in Florida wear. I can't help it, though. I look around her, and there in seat 16B is most definitely not a geriatric tourist, instead it's a striking man. A little older than me, but not enough to be a deal breaker. *Could this be fate?* No. *But what are the odds?* I can't stop myself from getting a little excited. We'd just been joking around about my Mr. Right being in 16B, and lo and behold—there he sits.

"Do you want to go through and do the seatbelt checks? Give a little extra yank on 16B's strap?" Lana asks me with an arched brow.

"Don't mind if I do." I straighten my shoulders and perk the girls up as I look down at my well-endowed bosom. When I get to 16B, I smile and tilt my head. He has sandy blond hair styled neat and clean, bright blue eyes, a strong jaw line, and perfect, pouty, kissable lips.

He gives me a panty-dropping crooked smile and says, "Hi. I can already tell this is going to be an enjoyable flight." Not wanting to make my interest in him too obvious, I smile and keep going, looking back over my shoulder as I brush past him. When I make it to the back of the plane, there's a few passengers still standing. Some putting luggage in the overhead bin and a few exiting the restrooms. One is an attractive blond in a short, bright yellow dress who lightly bumps into me as she exits.

"Excuse me." She giggles.

"Not a problem, ma'am."

I get a whiff of overpowering perfume, but it still doesn't cover the evident alcohol on her breath. *Great.* It's not uncommon for some people to drink a little to ease their nerves before a flight. It's when they go past the point of easing their nerves that problems happen. Let's hope this little ray of sunshine stays in her seat.

I tell her and other stray passengers to please find their seats because the plane is about to taxi.

After we go through safety precautions and are in air, Trip's soothing voice comes over the intercom. "Good afternoon, ladies and gentleman, this is your Supreme Commander, otherwise known as Captain Clynes."

I close my eyes and sigh. Captain Clynes goes through our cruising altitude and travel time. I wait for what Beatles song he will choose to sing. It used to only be "Lucy in the Sky with Diamonds," but ever since Kendall, his *someone*, he's been changing it up.

"Again, welcome aboard International Airlines." Then he begins singing today's chosen Beatles' song..." I Feel Fine."

Of course. As I listen to the lyrics I can easily tell why he chose that one. He bought her a diamond ring, they're in love and they feel fine. Would I feel fine if I was in love? I wouldn't know. I don't think I've ever truly been in love since I keep falling for these restless pilots. When we settle at a safe, cruising point Lana comes to me and smirks.

"Come on, Jo. Go through again and see how Mr. Hottie in 16B is doing."

"You're right. I do need to go check on the passengers. See if I can be of some *assistance*." *Instead of worrying about hunky pilots who are not available.* Not that I really want a relationship with Trip anymore. I just can't help but look at the idea longingly and want exactly what I don't have. Love.

When I'm almost to 16B, an elderly lady in 15B gets my attention. "I'm sorry, dear, but do you have blankets for purchase? I get cold very easily. I had a blanket, but I guess I forgot it. Ha. I can't keep up with anything anymore."

I smile. "Not a problem. I'll be right back."

Right as I'm turning to go retrieve a blanket, I hear a woman's voice speak. "Good thing I have you to keep me warm."

Still smiling, I turn back around to find 16B being cuddled next to the woman I saw earlier exiting the restrooms. *Sunshine. Or make that – Slutty Sunshine.* Her dress is riding dangerously high up her thigh. He doesn't meet my eyes, but she looks at me with an embarrassed giggle. Forcing my smile to remain in place, I spin on my heels to go retrieve the lady's blanket.

As I'm pushing the drink cart down the aisle, I come face to face with 16B and he's smirking at me.

ARROGANT ARRIVAL

The giggly woman next to him is now sleeping, and I can't help but notice they are both wearing gold bands on their left hands.

"Can I offer you a beverage, sir?"

He raises his eyebrows, "Did you know the human body is seventy-five percent water?"

"That's very interesting. Is there anything I can get you?"

"Well, I'm looking at a tall glass of water right now, and I'm very thirsty." Then he winks.

Oh God. He can't be serious. 16B just became Mr. Sleazy. Inwardly I cringe at how I actually thought this guy was hot not too long ago. "Would you like to wake your *wife* to see if she'd like a beverage?"

Both his eyebrows rise at that. I think I've put him in his place, but he shocks me further. "I've not known her to ever turn down a drink. Especially one that looks so fresh and sweet. We're open to trying anything." *Is he saying what I think he is?* "O-kay." I quickly open the bottle of water and pour two cups. Instead of handing them to him directly, I place them on the tray out of fear of accidently touching this guy and sending him the *wrong* signal. I'm so flustered, I almost don't realize I still have many more rows of passengers to service. Quickly, I finish offering drinks—actual drinks—to the rest of the plane and then rush to the back of the plane to Lana and Renee.

"16B is definitely *not* Mr. Right," I tell Lana and Renee. "Ugh...I'm so ready for this flight to be over."

"Don't give up hope, Jo. He'll come when you least expect it," Lana offers.

"Yeah. Think of it as he's experiencing a delay." Renee smiles.

"Hardy-har-har, ladies."

My life is experiencing a delay. I'm twenty-nine years old, and I feel like despite constantly being on the go, my life has gone nowhere. This is the last year of my twenties. I should be living it up. Instead, I'm sitting on standby just waiting for something to happen.

Looking back, I've traveled to places most people only dream of going, been around the world more times than I can count, but what's the point of the adventure when you're completely alone?

CHAPTER 2

Jimmy

"Jimmy! How was your flight?" Bianca's cheerful voice comes through the speaker.

"Great. The plane handled really well."

"Thank you so much for flying the plane down for Dex's friend. I'm sorry to have called you on such short notice."

"Short notice? You gave me a week. I don't think you understand that my job is usually on the same schedule as fly by the seat of my pants is. Pun intended."

"Well, Dex and I both appreciate it. Thank you."

"Thank you for getting me a first-class ticket back. I usually fly economy when I go commercial, so that was a pleasant surprise."

"Dex offered to have someone come get you. You could've flown private, ya know."

"Nah. It'll be nice to have some company for a change. Besides, I'm taking a moment to eat. Chocolate shake and cheeseburger heading my way any minute."

"Chocolate shake and cheeseburger?"

"Yup. My favorites."

"Hey, I'll have to call you back. Georgina is in my makeup again."

"Awe. Let her have it."

"Says the man who doesn't have to clean her and it up. Bye, Jim." Bianca laughs.

"Bye, Bianca." I end the call and place my phone face down on the table in the airport restaurant. I have about three hours until my flight from Miami takes me back to New York, so I've got time to kill and people to watch.

"And then the asshole had the nerve to wink." My ears perk up at hearing the angry woman's voice. Out of my peripheral vision, I can see three dark-haired ladies, all in flight attendant attire sitting at the table next to mine. Geez, they almost look like triplets.

"So what did you say?" one of the women asks.

"What could I say? I wanted to run my cart over his foot. Instead, I smiled and asked if he wanted to wake his *wife* up to see if she would like anything to drink."

"Just goes to show you." The one across from her shakes her head.

"Yeah, that *all* men are assholes." The angry one grumbles.

"Dicks."

"Jerks."

Not able to stop myself, I mumble under my own breath. "Bastards." I notice the table next to me has gone silent. Biting my bottom lip, I turn my head and sure enough, they heard me. Throwing a hand up, I smile. "Sorry. Didn't mean to eavesdrop. Couldn't help but agree with all of your... assessments."

ARROGANT ARRIVAL

Luckily, my waitress arrives with my plate. Their food arrives as well. I grab a fry and nod to the three women. "Enjoy your meal, ladies." I take a bite of the fry I'm holding and try to focus on my meal and ignore them shooting daggers my way.

The ladies then lower their voices to a whisper as they continue their conversation. I watch a couple struggle to get through the airport with a rowdy toddler. I can't help but smile remembering family vacations with my parents because that was me, I used to always run off. I couldn't get to the planes fast enough. I loved flying. I've always wanted to be a pilot for as long as I can remember.

I look through my phone messages for my next flights I have booked. I'm twenty-five and a self-employed contract pilot, but I work for another private company part time. They pay me a monthly salary to be available certain days to fly their employees and CEOs here and there. Then I work for myself taking on jobs that interest me. Today, I was delivering a plane from New York to Miami for a friend of my cousin's husband, Mr. Moneybags, Dex Truitt. *Her name for him, not mine.* Anyway, it's a pretty sweet gig, and even though I'm rarely home, my schedule is pretty much my own.

Just then, I notice two of the ladies stand up. One of them pats the one still sitting on the shoulder. "We have to catch our flight. I wish we were working this leg together, Jo."

The one who's remained seated smiles. It's a beautiful smile, even if it is weak. Something about her tugs at my heart strings. I want to see a genuine smile from her. She keeps her attempted, obviously fake smile in place as she watches her friends gather their belongings. "Me too. You girls try not to get into any trouble."

The one standing across from her smirks. "A layover in Vegas, what trouble could we possibly get into? Can you say strip clubs?"

"Oh my God, you wouldn't?" Her smile stretches a little more right before she buries her face in her hands. "Oh, you definitely would, you trollop."

They all three burst into fits of giggles, and I can't help but nod in agreement. That *does* sound like a good time. The other two make their exit, leaving the beauty sitting alone. I know I should keep my mouth shut, but it's not in my nature to be silent.

"Rough flight?"

She looks up and I'm floored by those gorgeous, big brown eyes. I take a moment to examine the beauty before me—no, more like complete knockout. Her lips are slightly full, midnight black hair, sharp cheekbones, and beautiful golden skin. She has a long, slender neck and dainty fingers. Her eyes are so dark, but there's a fire burning behind them. Her face appears so stern, but I can see through her mask. She's hurting. She needs to laugh, let loose, most assuredly get laid.

"I don't know. Ever been asked by someone to have a threesome?" I tilt my head and raise my eyebrows. *I mean*...before I can answer, she continues. "With an older man *and his wife*?"

"Oh...this happened while *in* flight?" I can't help but grin as I ask. She purses her lips and nods. "That's one kinky mile high club you're involved in. What airline is this? I may need to change my flight."

ARROGANT ARRIVAL

She gives a half-hearted chuckle. "Well, to be honest, I said they offered. I didn't say I obliged."

"That's funny." When she continues to frown, I sigh. "C'mon. You're not letting one pervy couple get you down."

"Technically, I don't know if the wife was game. She was asleep."

"So you asked if you could get him anything and he..."

"Basically, yeah. With his wife's head asleep on his shoulder. Zero shame in his game, I guess."

"Can you blame a guy for fantasizing? I shrug and take a bite of my burger.

"You know what, I'm done. I can see right now what kind of guy you are." She goes back to focusing on her food. It was a joke. This woman is wound up way too tight. The overwhelming need to do something about this has me picking up my plate of food and milkshake and going over to her table. Her eyes widened as I sit across from her and slurp my milkshake. She scoffs and holds her hand out. "Yes, by all means, please join me after I said I was done speaking with you."

"I take offense at that little remark. But since you asked so nicely." I take a long slurp from my straw. "I believe everyone deserves a second chance at redemption, so here's me giving you yours." I wink.

"You're too kind." She deadpans.

"I know." I take my straw and stir my milkshake, ignoring her obvious sarcasm while doing my damndest to try and make her smile. I wiggle my eyebrows and smirk.

"And humble." She mocks surprise.

"I won't argue that. Next, are you going to say handsome?"

"Nope." She says that while popping the P for emphasis. "I'd planned on skipping right over that lil' gem and diving straight into arrogant," she clips.

"Hey!" I sit up straighter, my hand across my chest as I feign hurt.

"Are you going to argue *that* assessment?" She smirks. It's not the genuine smile I was going for, but it's definitely a genuine smirk. And fuck me, do I love it.

"Nope. But I most certainly don't have to like it. By the way, when's your next flight?"

"In two hours." She goes back to eating her salad, and I can't help but admire how her lips wrap around her fork.

"Fate is on your side, then." I pick up my burger and smile widely at her before I take a bite and say, "My flight doesn't leave for another two-and-a-half hours so I'm all yours."

"You're right. Fate is most assuredly on my side. That extra half hour means that we're not on the same flight. I couldn't imagine what I'd have had to do in a previous life to get two shitty flights back to back."

"Ouch." I chuckle. "You definitely don't hold back, huh?" I like this woman. She's feisty. But she's clearly still upset, and I'm thinking it's not because of anything I've said or done. "I was just thinking… you're clearly upset over something bigger than just a guy propositioning you. I mean, let's be honest, you're gorgeous. This can't be the first time, and it won't be the last. In fact, I bet you'll be propositioned again real soon." I give her a crooked smile, still trying to get a smile out of her.

ARROGANT ARRIVAL

"Real soon?" She fights back a smile. *Almost. I see her fighting it.*

I lean back in my chair and grin. Lowering my voice, I promise. "Real soon."

"Well, if I didn't accept that one, it's not likely I'm going to accept the next one."

"Ah," I hold up a finger. "Hear me out on this. What if fate has brought you here for a reason? Think about it? What are the odds that you'd be sitting right here with me with time to kill? Time to help you get over whatever it is that's bothering you. And," I place my elbows on the table and lean forward, "I guarantee you'll get over whatever it is. In fact, I bet you'll have a damn good connecting flight because you'll still be sore in the best way from getting over it – or under it."

A surprised chuckle escapes her. "I don't even know what to say to that!"

"Say yes, I mean, it's really the only answer." I cross my arms, hoping my bulging biceps and the way my button-up shirt stretches will seal the deal.

"Wow. Let me see if I get what you're offering?" The way she squints her eyes at me tells me I may not have, in fact, won her over...and now I'm a bit scared. "You're offering to solve my problems with sex?" *Basically.* "Pretty sure everyone knows—correction, every *female* knows—that that doesn't solve any problems. Sex complicates more than it helps."

"Well, aren't you in a sour mood. What I'm proposing is that a few minutes with me and you'll be higher than any flight you've ever been on." I stretch out my hands, and give a one-shoulder shrug. "Your solution has arrived." I spread my arms out farther for her to feast her eyes on all that is the miracle named Jimmy.

"All I can say is wouldn't that be a very arrogant arrival."

"I prefer confident." She shakes her head, so I continue as I let my arms fall and challenge her. "Only one way to prove me wrong?" I tilt my head with a smile.

"That's not going to work. I'm not worried about proving you wrong because that would insinuate that I care...when I don't." And with that, she stands up and sashays away.

I pick up my milkshake and sulk as I take a long slurp. I watch her hips sway in her fitted uniform. I call out, "Now who's being arrogant?"

Jolene

Despite myself, I silently giggle as I walk away from the gorgeous yet ridiculous man at my table. I'm definitely adding an extra sway to my stride for good measure. If I was on a layover, I might actually take the cocky stranger up on his offer. I wouldn't have to worry about getting hurt because I'd never see him again. No fears of getting attached. Best of all, he's not a pilot, so I don't run the risk of getting hurt again or having to look him in the face anytime in the near future.

I'm halfway to my gate when my phone dings with a text message. That's never a good sign when you get messaged while you are in an airport. Standing at

ARROGANT ARRIVAL

the gate, I swipe the screen and curse. A bad storm is approaching so my flight has been canceled. I'm stuck in Miami until tomorrow morning for my next shift. Damn. I turn around to make my way toward arrivals and baggage claim. My next order of business is to find a cab and check in at one of the hotels the airline provides for us.

I've just stepped on the escalator when I feel someone step on behind me. A low voice leans down and speaks in my ear as the escalator descends. "Now you can't deny that this is fate."

A gasp escapes me as I turn my neck to look up. "I'm sure that's every stalker's favorite line."

His deep chuckle causes me to have butterflies in my stomach. I watch as he stands up straighter. "Stalker? Me? I bet you heard that my flight was canceled so you were rushing to transportation in hopes of finding me. You knew I'd need to have a room for the night and that rooms were going to be few and far between with all flights being grounded and were most likely planning to offer to keep me company." The mischievous gleam in his blue eyes is so playful yet heated. His perfectly straight white smile screams of naughty promises. I allow my eyes to take in my sexy stranger as we ride down the escalator—medium build, black hair, blue eyes that have a hint of green, straight nose, dark facial hair that's trimmed close, providing the makings for a very nice five o'clock shadow, and olive skin. No wedding ring or indentation where one used to be...that's a good sign, at least. And to complete the package, he's wearing a white button up and navy slacks.

"Do I pass your inspection?"

I fight back a smile at being caught sizing him up. "Just barely."

"As long as I pass." We step off the escalator and he falls in step with me.

I side-eye him and ask, "Do you have any baggage?"

"Whoa, you don't mess around, little lady. Oddly enough, I like it. Come clean from the get go. I mean, usually I wait to see if there's going to be a second date because I like to discuss these matters in private."

"And by *in private* you mean not in *baggage* claim?" I can't help smiling at him.

"Huh? Oh!" He gives me a sheepish smile and that's it, I'm done for. "No, I don't have any baggage. You?"

"I have everything with me." I take a step closer to him and lower my voice. "I think I have everything I'll need for the night."

He takes a step closer toward me, erasing any space there was between us. "Then let's go? I booked a room as soon as they announced my flight was canceled. Will you at least join me for dinner?"

I lick my bottom lip and don't miss how his eyes darken watching me. "I don't even know your name."

"Hello, Jo, my name is Jim."

My eyes widen and I take a step back. "You really are a stalker. How'd you know my name?"

"I was eavesdropping, remember?" He takes another step forward, leaving no space between us again. "Your friend said Jo."

"It's actually Jolene."

"Well, I want us to be friendly, so I'll call you Jo." He takes my hand in his. "I want to get to know you a lot better...Jo." His eyes search mine. I bite my bottom lip trying to fight the smile. When I see his goofy, megawatt smile, I lose the battle. "There it is. No matter what else happens, for the rest of the night I'll be a satisfied man. I've been wanting to see you actually smile and mean it since I first saw you."

I roll my eyes and look off. *This guy is laying it on thick*. He tugs my hand to get my full attention back on him. "You have the most beautiful smile. And that's not just a line. It was worth chasing you through an airport."

"You're such a stalker. Do you hear yourself?"

"Nobody's perfect."

I can't help but laugh. "Nobody's perfect? Not sure I should leave the building with a stalker, Jim."

"Probably not the safest and best decision. Let's just share a cab...to the same place...and maybe go to the same restaurant, sit at the same table and eat dinner together? We already shared part of a lunch together. That you didn't even finish."

I study him. I've been around a lot of people with my job. I've learned a lot about people as well. He honestly seems like a good guy. I don't have to sleep with him, but I already know I might. I can study him some more over dinner.

"Fine."

He smiles and gently tugs me toward the automatic doors. He tells me he'll order us a ride through the app on his phone, and then we're quiet. I should be worried about getting into a strange vehicle with a strange man, hell, possibly two strange men if the driver of the car is male. I'm pulled from my worry by the sounds of taxis honking and people talking around us. I've already made up my mind. I'm about to have a one-night stand with this complete stranger I picked up in the airport. Or did he pick me up? This is crazy! And reckless! Sure, I've had hookups with coworkers, but I knew them. Okay…some I didn't know that well. I'm certifiably insane. I decide to leave a text for Lana and Renee. They're working so they may not get it, but at least there will be a trail of evidence should I go missing.

> Me: If I die or come up missing, this is the man I was last with.

Discreetly, I take a photo of Jim standing there. He doesn't look like a Jim, honestly. I don't know what a Jim looks like, but he seems like he should have a more interesting name. Something exotic. Like Phoenix or Lachlan or some other multi-syllabic concoction of letters.

> Me: His name is Jim.
> Renee: OMFG! He is HOTT!
> Lana: WAIT! Is that the guy from the restaurant?
> Me: Yes. Aren't y'all up in the air yet?
> Renee: I guess things got interesting after we left…
> Lana: We have a connecting flight in Atlanta. What's his last name? First name and a pic won't help if you go missing.

"Jim?" He turns to look at me. "What's your last name?"

ARROGANT ARRIVAL

"Georgakopolous."

What? "Georg-a-what-po-los? Hold on. Your name is Jim, which is like the most average name compared to John, and your last name is a complete mouthful."

He tilts his head and smirks. "You're right, I am a complete mouthful. At least from what I've been told. In that area, I guarantee my inspection will pass with flying colors."

I roll my eyes but continue to check him out. He does seem rather promising. I clear my throat and ask, "What kind of last name is that?"

"Greek."

"Greek? You're Jim the Greek?" He does look Greek now that he mentions it. Tan complexion, strong straight nose, sexy wavy black hair and thick eyebrows. His eyelashes are so dark that he looks like he's wearing mascara. *Lucky bastard.* Those stunning blue eyes pop against the dark contrasting colors. I bet he wakes up looking this fantastic. *One way to find out...*

Where Jim seems like such a simple name, his last name makes up for it the lack of intrigue in the first-name department. Maybe his parents felt sorry for him having to learn to spell that last name, so they wanted to keep his first name short and sweet.

"Or Jimmy the Greek." He smiles and I almost wonder if he's playing me. I narrow my eyes because he has that mischievous look again. He lets out a low chuckle and explains, "My real name is Dimitrios."

Whoa. He has an accent when he pronounces his name. Holy. Mother. Of. God... *Where the hell did that come from?* I'm ready to drop my panties right now, right outside of airport transportation!

"Jim comes from that. It's like James, in English." He speaks with an American accent now. How does he switch so easily back and forth and so casual? Would it be weird for me to ask him to only speak with the Greek accent for the rest of our time together? Too creepy? All I know is that my handsome stranger is bilingual…and it's sexy as fuck. I need to get a grip though and pretend to display a certain amount of dignity.

"Ummm, I don't hear how Jim comes from Dimitrios."

"True and I don't hear how it comes from James." Point made. He smiles. "In Greek it's *Jimmy*." The way he pronounces the 'J' has more of a 'G' sound, and with that intonation I can hear the similarity more. My phone buzzes again.

> Renee: Hello?
> Me: Sorry. He goes by Jim but his full name is Dimitrios Georgakopolous.
> Lana: Oh shit. Did you take off with a sexy Greek god?
> Me: Apparently.
> Renee: Let us know if he really is a god in the bedroom!

"Here's our ride." Jim tells me and gently places a hand on the small of my back.

> Me: I've got to go! I'll text you what hotel we're staying at.
> Renee: I want more details than that!
> Lana: Be safe!

ARROGANT ARRIVAL

I plan to be safe, with my life and my heart. But I also plan to have amazing sex with a Greek god.

CHAPTER 3

Jimmy

We arrive to the hotel and I open the door for her. I go to the front desk to check in while Jolene stands back in the main area of the lobby.

"I have you for a king-size bed, staying one night, correct?"

A gentleman would request two queens just in case Jolene needs a room. I could offer her to stay in mine... in two separate beds of course. I look back over at the striking woman standing in the middle of the lobby...

"Sure, sounds perfect."

I'm most definitely not a gentleman. I do go the extra mile and get two key cards just in case she takes me up on my offer. Let's face it, if she does take me up on the offer, we won't need them since neither of us will be leaving the room. I stroll toward her and she smiles at me. *Damn, that smile.* She could make a saint have devilish thoughts. She's almost as tall as me and her flight uniform accents all her lovely curves. That raven colored hair looks silky and I'm dying to let it

ARROGANT ARRIVAL

loose from that bun so I can run my fingers through it. She's standing so stiff, but I've seen her fire. Now I'm ready to see if I can feel her heat and get burned in the best way by her.

"All checked in?" Her eyes are wide but guarded.

"Yup. What do you say to room service?"

"You said to join you for dinner at the hotel restaurant." She narrows those bronze eyes at me, but I see a slight waver.

"I did." I agree. "But then a thought occurred to me."

"Uh-huh. And what's that?"

I stand closer to where there's only a breath between our chests. Leaning down, I whisper in her ear, "I'm not sure the restaurant would approve of us dining in our underwear?"

"To be fair, I'm not sure *I* would either." She turns her face up toward mine. We're so close that I could easily kiss her right now. One inch closer and our lips would touch.

"Really? Well, if you'd rather have no underwear, I'm game if you are. You're my guest, after all. I want you to be comfortable."

Jolene pushes past me and begins walking toward the sign of the restaurant. "I'll be comfortable dining in the restaurant dressed as we are." She calls out to me as she keeps walking.

"That works too," I grumble under my breath.

Seated in a tiny corner of the restaurant, Jolene leans her chin on her delicate hand. "So, where are you from, Jim the Greek?"

"New York City, Bayside. You?"

"Tampa, Florida. Do you travel a lot?" "Quite a bit. I have since I was a kid. Clearly, you do. Ever go anywhere just for fun,

not work related?"

"No. I work a lot so I haven't had enough time. You obviously know what I do for a

living, what do you do?"

Before I can answer, the waitress arrives to take our order. When she leaves, Jolene eyes me and continues her line of questioning. "Tell me, Jim, is this typical for you?"

"Yes. Typically, I order steak. I do love my beef."

"Noooo," She draws out. I grin, pleased with myself, watching her fight back a smile. "I meant picking up women at the airport."

I chuckle. "No. Actually, this is a first. What about you? Do you typically leave with a man you met at the airport?" Her smile vanishes, letting me know immediately that I've said the wrong thing. "Hey, I'm not judging." She asked first, in my defense. "Let's discuss chicken. Do you typically prefer poultry dishes?"

She giggles. *Thank God that worked.* "Poultry dishes?"

"Of the poultry variety?"

"Although I appreciate your attempt at changing the subject, it's fine. Actually, it was typical for me to leave the airport with someone. Usually, it was a pilot." She scoffs. "It *was* a pilot. Always."

"That makes sense. More sense than scanning for stranded, lonely travelers while they drink their chocolate shakes."

ARROGANT ARRIVAL

"I think I'd prefer the lonely traveler than the pilot. I've recently made a vow to never date a pilot again."

Oh shit. "Let me make sure one thing is clear. You never want to *date* a pilot again? Because that's been your typical type?"

"Exactly. Never again. I'd walk through fire to *not* date a pilot ever again."

The waitress places a cocktail in front of Jolene and a beer in front of me. I release a nervous chuckle, "Fire, huh? Rather have flames lick your body rather than the tongue of a pilot?"

"Yes."

"What if it was an extremely sexy pilot? With a skillful tongue? Who could make you feel on fire in the best way."

Jolene picks up her cocktail glass and looks at me over the rim. "Sounds like you want to sleep with a pilot." She takes a sip and then places her glass back down. "I know exactly how skillful their tongues are... with lies."

"That's most people. Unfortunately." I take a long drink from my beer. I lick my lips and lean on the table. I focus on those gorgeous, pouty lips and liquid, honey eyes that are illuminated by the fire burning inside of her. Her shoulders are tense and her back is straight as a board, it has me wanting to pull her out of her chair and do something wild. Maybe kissing her in the middle of this restaurant? Maybe knocking everything off the table and sitting her on top of it like they do in the movies? Maybe...pulling her on top of my lap and telling her to buckle up because it could be a bumpy ride. *Oh God.* That was a bad line, even for me.

"Are you like most people?" Her voice brings me out of my crazy scenarios. I stare at her with raised eyebrows. She repeats the question. "Are you like most people, Jim the Greek?"

We're not dating. This isn't a date... technically. It's hopefully a great night of sex. There's no reason to tell her. None at all. Guilt gnaws at my gut, but then she bats those eyelashes at me. I take a long drink from my beer while maintaining eye contact with her. The heat burning in her eyes has my body on fire. "Let's go to the room and I can show you *exactly* how I'm *not* like most people?"

That came off really cocky, but damn it, I can deliver. I am fully prepared to make this a night she won't forget. I'll spend all night loosening every tense muscle in her delectable body.

She smirks and tilts her head. In a sweet voice feigning innocence, she says, "That's right. You booked a room, didn't you?"

I sure as hell did. "I'll tell them our room number and ask them to send our order up."

"Tell them they can take their time. I've got an appetite for something else."

My guilt over my career details has been replaced by something else. A much stronger emotion—lust.

I'm not a complete scumbag, though. *I'll tell her the truth – if she asks me directly. Again.*

Jolene

Jim scans his keycard and then holds the door open for me to enter. I pull my carry on behind me and shimmy past him. Jim walks over to the night-stand. Not wanting to waste any time, I place my carry on against the wall and turn to face him. I open my mouth to speak, but stop when the room fills with oldies music. *Oh boy. I know how to pick 'em. This night keeps getting more strange.*

My eyebrows pull together and I debate if I should run. "Setting the mood?"

He leans his shoulder against the wall, watching me with his hands in the pockets of his slacks. "Elvis Presley does have one of the sexiest voices of all time."

"Ah. Elvis fan. I used to know a guy who was a huge Beatles fan."

"Yeah, it took four of them to compete with the King. Besides, this song is fitting, don't you think?"

I listen to Elvis' soulful voice croon about it being *now or never* and *who knows when we'll meet again*. Jim the Greek is an Elvis fan, who would've guessed? I can get on board. I allow the music to course through me and feel the beat. Slowly, I unbutton the top of my uniform blazer. Jim's eyes seem to shine brighter. I continue to slowly unbutton my top without breaking eye contact because if I did, my nerves would be on full display. When I've finished unbuttoning my blazer, I slide out of it and toss it on the chair. Then, I start on my white button up. When the buttons have cleared my chest, revealing my white lace bra, I can see Jim's obvious excitement when I give him a complete once over. *Yup. Looks like he is going to pass that inspection with flying colors.*

I toss my shirt and then reach behind my back, making sure to perk my girls up in the process as I then go to unzip my long skirt. I let the skirt drop to the floor and step out, wearing only my matching white lace undies and navy heels.

"Allow me to be of assistance." Jim steps in front of me, placing a hand on my shoulder. He gently pushes me to sit on the edge of the bed. God, is it wrong that I'm *hearing* him say that in that delicious Greek accent?

"Now you want to help?" I ask him in a taunting tone as I raise one eyebrow.

Instead of keeping our banter going, his face is serious as he wraps a strong hand on my calf and slides it down to my heel. He pushes the shoe off and does the same to my other foot. Jim places a hand on my chest and gently guides me to lie back on the bed. Hooking his fingers through my underwear, he drags the lace material down and tosses them to the side. My body jerks when he places a sensual kiss on my bellybutton. I gasp as he goes lower, lower, and *lower*. He was right. Heat spreads through my veins and my body does feel like it's on fire. Fisting my hands in the white sheets, my legs wrap around his back needing to keep him anchored to me.

"*Jim.*" I gasp. I want more but I don't know if I can handle more.

He raises up and my eyes lock on his dilated pupils with blue and green swirls. Slowly, his tongue slides across his glistening lips, evidence of my arousal causing me to suck in a deep breath. His voice sounds deep and strained as he growls, "You like that?"

"Wh-what do you think?" I pant as I raise up slightly.

ARROGANT ARRIVAL

The arrogant ass actually winks and gives me a cocky smirk. Before I can make a snarky remark, I feel his teeth nip me. I shriek but then I feel his warm tongue there. I couldn't form words if my life depended on it. Pressure begins building, and I feel my body climbing higher and higher. A scream begins to build in my throat, so I grab a pillow and cover my face. I tighten my legs around him and squeeze as I ride out the most intense orgasm.

I open my eyes to find Jim still gripping my thighs and breathing heavy. He's staring at me, and despite his face just being there, I feel a little self-conscious. He cuts those piercing blue eyes to me, and in a breathy voice says, "I think we can get you to come harder."

Harder? I don't think... He slides his arms under my thighs and holds me tight in a firm grip. Not taking his eyes off mine, he slowly lowers his mouth, and then...*Oh God!* He most definitely delivered on his promise because now I'm seeing stars. Why did I ever waste time with those asshole pilots over the years when I should've been looking for a Greek man named Jim?

Jimmy

I force myself to stop. I could devour this woman all night, but the taste of her, combined with her tightening her legs around me and panting my name, I'm going to blow in my pants. My pride will not allow for that. Plus, I'd never forgive myself if I didn't get to experience all of her. I push myself off the bed to stand. Jolene's chest rises and falls. She's still wearing a bra, I'll need to fix that very soon.

Quickly, I begin unbuttoning my shirt. I'm so excited that my hands are shaking. I can't get to her fast enough. The heat behind Jolene's eyes is almost an inferno. She crawls toward me on the bed. Her eyes search my face before she crashes her lips to mine. Her fingers work in a rush to help undo the buttons. I shake out of my shirt, while Jolene bites my bottom lip as she undoes my pants. As soon as my arms are free from my shirt, I wrap them around her and we fall on the bed together. The music has stopped. Our heavy breathing and skin touching are the only sounds we make.

There's the fire I knew was burning inside of her. This woman is all passion right now. There's no sign of stiffness, other than her nipples are hard as rocks. The feel of her warm skin against mine sends a blaze through me. I can't get enough of her. I can't get close enough, I can't taste her enough, I can't move fast enough, yet I want to slow down and savor her...but I can't, the need is too great, me wanting to sink into her tight heat my sole focus right now. She moans into my mouth and that's my undoing.

"Fuck. I forgot the condom in my pants."

It hurts to pull away from her, but I hurry and grab a condom from my wallet on the floor. Ripping the packet apart with my teeth, I take out the condom and slide it on. I crawl back on top of Jolene and take her hands in mine, holding them above her head.

"Are you ready?" I let out with a heavy breath. Her gorgeous smile and eyes are bright with excitement as she nods and pulls me closer, my green light to go all the way with this beautiful woman. With a single thrust, we become one, and I silently thank God for sending that storm. Our hands squeeze each other's as I begin to move. Her legs hold me against her, pulling me in deeper with each thrust as I lean down to kiss her neck. She raises her chin up, granting me more access as she moans and I greedily feast on her. I go back up to her lips, but she's having none of that as she pushes me off, forces me on my back and down on the pillow.

Holy fuck. Jolene straddles me and now I'm back inside her. It's better than any fantasy I've ever dreamed up. "You're a fucking goddess."

"I guess I'd have to be to keep up with a Greek god?"

I reach up and finally remove her bra. I chuckle, "I actually feel like one getting to have you." My hands get their fill, but I can't resist, the need to taste her more is so great.

"Tasting you." I sit up with Jolene still straddling me and take one of her perky breasts between my lips. I move to the other breast and hold her tight against me with one hand, while my other slides down, squeezing her ass and encouraging her to keep up that delicious friction and speed. Her nails scrape my scalp as she grabs at my hair, running her hands through each strand. I jerk and adjust to go in deeper while I hold her firmly on top of me.

"Being inside you...I've never felt this good." I grunt and pump harder. Jolene reaches up and undoes her bun that's already coming loose. I fall back against the pillow and marvel at her beauty and how she takes control. The sight of her hair falling down while she rides me is embarrassingly my undoing.

"*Jolene,*" I growl as I quickly flip her over and position her on her hands and knees. I power into her. She screams out as her knuckles turn white gripping the sheets. My eyelids grow heavy as I feel her body constrict around me. As the sweet sound of her moan hits my ears, I don't want to miss the look on her face as she comes. I flip her back over and swiftly slide back in. Her eyes squeeze shut, and I worry I'm being too rough, but she pulls me closer and releases another whimper of pleasure. *Those rewarding sweet sounds will be my undoing.* It's also another green light for me, so I ramp up my movements. My eyes open and meets hers as we both come apart in each other's arms.

Neither one of us says anything. I don't even know what to say after that. This was supposed to be a one-night stand, but that didn't feel like anything I'd ever had before. How? She's a stranger to me, but I swear that was not just sex...not at all. It was a real connection. Part of me is terrified. I need to get up and get as far away from this as I can. But another part of me, the caveman who is obviously in touch with his emotions, wants to feel that again. She can't leave me tonight, not when I need more. So much more.

CHAPTER 4

Jolene

What the hell just happened? What was that? I've never in my life experienced such a mind-blowing orgasm like that. Wait...correction, multiple mind-blowing orgasms. Honestly, I'm a little freaked out. This was supposed to just be a night to let loose and break my pattern of hooking up with pilots. It wasn't supposed to be serious but—that—that felt serious! Too serious, if I'm being honest.

"Hey," Jim whispers as he runs his strong hand through my hair and then down my cheek. "You're tensing up on me, and not in the good, moaning my name way like earlier."

When I smile, he smiles back even wider. "Sorry. It was...nothing."

"It was far from nothing. I know," I watch his throat as he swallows. He licks his lips and then continues, "I felt it too. That was intense."

"Yeah," I whisper. I feel better knowing he felt it too. I shift underneath him and start to raise up, but his hand gently guides me back down.

"Don't leave. Whatever you're thinking, don't go. Stay the night."

My eyes search his normally playful eyes that are now serious and pleading. I nod and he gives me that mega-watt smile again. Immediately, his eyes turn bright and sparkle with naughty promises. "You still haven't eaten your dinner. I'm sure room service will be here any minute, so you have to stick around. Besides, it'd be rude to love me and leave me."

I giggle but stop when I see how he's staring at me. "What?"

"I love your laugh." I'm at a loss for words. I feel slightly uncomfortable with how he is watching me. He frowns and says, "Well, don't stop because I said something."

"Now it's weird. I can't just laugh for no reason."

"Sure, you can." Jim then attacks me, his hands tickling me all over.

"Quit!" I beg between fits of laughter. "I swear, I'm going to pee myself!"

If I pee myself right now, I'd die. Jim, on the other hand, thinks this is hilarious and doesn't let up. To torture me further, he gets on top of me and pins me with his weight. One of his hands tickles me in all my ticklish places, while another hand tickles me in my most *sensitive* of places. "Oh...my...gosh," I gasp and giggle. I'm so confused with myself right now. "I... will..." I gasp and then squeak out, "hurt you!" I try to kick and punch him because I seriously can't stand to be tickled. Over our laughter, I can barely hear the knock at the door. "Jim," I giggle out, "the...door!"

"Room service," a voice calls out.

ARROGANT ARRIVAL

He quickly inserts two fingers and presses right where he needs to with his thumb. I gasp as a shock courses through my body. "Coming," he calls out and winks at me. He jumps off the bed before I can wipe that smug grin off his face with my foot. I take advantage of this opportunity to admire his backside. I used to wonder in history class if those Greek statutes were modeled after real men. Jim definitely could've been a model. His ass looks perfectly carved from smooth marble.

"If you want me to answer the door, I suggest you stop eye fucking me...before I crawl back up there and give you your...what are we up to, third? Or is the fourth orgasm of the night?"

I scoff. "Oh, puh-please. I wasn't even looking at you. You're so full of yourself."

He slides his slacks back on with a look, letting me know he knows I'm full of shit, and goes to the door.

My stomach growls when I get a whiff of the delicious aroma coming from the open door. I won't admit it to Jim, but he really gave me a work out. He comes back to the bed with a tray. I wrap a sheet around me and accept the plate of food he hands me.

"We're going to eat in bed?" I ask.

Jim unbuttons his slacks and slides them off. Then he unashamedly sits criss-cross next to me, "Yup. Remember, you said you didn't want to eat in our underwear? So," he makes a point of looking down at his nudity, "no underwear."

I bite the inside of my cheek. *Smartass*. He better be glad he's so hot and good in bed. I don't think any woman could put up with him otherwise.

After we finish our main course, Jim takes a spoonful of cheesecake and brings it to my lips. I sigh as the creamy goodness touches my tongue. He watches me, and I know what that sound does to him. I fully intend on picking up where we left off only moments ago—well, not the tickling moment. Although, I can understand now where people might enjoy a little torture with their pleasure. Outside, we can hear the heavy rain hitting the window as the thunder and lightning put on a light and sound show in the distance, and for once, I'm so grateful my flight was canceled. How else would I have ended up in bed while a gorgeous man feeds me cheesecake? I deliberately slide my tongue across my lips slowly, pretending to lick off crumbs. Jim's eyes burn bright blue and his nostrils flare. I take the spoon from him and offer him a bite. I get another spoonful and bring it close to his lips. I watch as they part, but instead of placing the spoon into his mouth, I whip it around into mine. His eyes widen so much that it's comical. He releases a low growl. I smirk and dramatically moan.

"Oh! I'm sorry. Did you want some more?"

He takes the box between us and sits it on the nightstand. In an eerily calm, low voice, he whispers, "Oh, I want some more." I let out a surprised yelp as he grabs my ankles and pulls to where I'm lying flat on my back. "I'm not finished." He crawls up the bed and licks my thighs. "Not even close." He licks the other thigh. "You're a full-course meal. And now it's time for the main course."

The next morning, I stretch and relish the pleasant ache from my worked muscles. Jim wraps his arm

ARROGANT ARRIVAL

around me and nuzzles my neck. It's nice waking up next to someone and feeling their warmth. It was very nice last night having my body feel cherished. In fact, I'm going to be sore all day from all the cherishing.

Outside, the rain is still coming down heavy. I grab my phone off the table next to the bed.

> Lana: Hello? Are you still alive?
> Renee: She's not answering us either because A.) He is a Greek sex god and she's been struck by his lightning bolt or B.) He was never Greek, just a psycho who lured her away, and we are horrible friends for encouraging her to get laid by a stranger... in the airport.
> Lana: Still not answering. JO! Where are you? We've literally flown half way across the country and still haven't heard from you.
> Renee: I was just joking...but now I'm nervous. Seriously, Jo, Lana and I are together yet still texting in this group message but we've been talking about you. If you don't answer us, we're calling the police.
> Lana: If you don't want hotel security or the police to burst through your door and see you naked, message us NOW.
> Renee: I'm tempted to call now because I'm pissed off. Answer us! I need to know you're alive, and if you are—I want details.
> Renee: The suspense is killing me...I hate you. I hope you're alive, but I really hate you.

Oh my gosh! I check the time of the messages. Last message was sent an hour ago. I begin typing, but then the room phone rings. Jim stirs and groans. I reach over and hurry to answer so I don't wake him. I'm also not quite ready for the awkward morning-after conversation with Jim.

"Hello?" I whisper into the phone.

"You bitch! We've been worried sick!" I can't help but burst out laughing at Renee's outburst. I can hear Lana in the background. "She answered?"

"I'm sorry. I *just* woke up." I release a little moan as I stretch while still lying in bed.

"Uh-huh. I see." Renee's voice perks up. "My-my. Some night, I take it?"

"You could say that," I coo into the phone and then giggle.

"Well, he must've really been good. I can't remember the last time I heard you this giddy. I guess I can forgive you for worrying us to death."

"I'm sorry." I hope my voice conveys my sincerity.

"Just don't do it again, promise?"

"I promise."

Next, Lana's voice comes in through the phone. "We have to go. Please keep us updated, and we demand all the naughty, filthy details. You owe us that much."

"How did you even find me?"

Lana scoffs. "Duh. You told us which hotel and his name. Wasn't that hard. I'm your sister, by the way, who's at the hospital with a baby. Just in case anyone asks."

"Well, take care, sis, and give my niece a kiss on the cheek for me."

ARROGANT ARRIVAL

"I had a boy! You have a nephew. Gosh, you're a horrible aunt—and sister—for not answering your phone."

"Oh, I'm so sorry since you never specified the gender of our fictional baby. I wish I would've known, I'd have sent a gift. Anyway, you two be safe and take care."

"You too! And answer your phone, or we'll find you!"

I reach over and hang up the phone, laughing at what crazy, but loyal, friends I have. I pick up my cell and check flight statuses since the rain doesn't look like it's letting up. Sure enough, all morning flights have been postponed until this afternoon when they hope the storm will clear.

Jim's gravelly voice sounds extra seductive this morning as he whispers in my ear. "There's absolutely no reason to get out of bed."

My stomach tightens and heat throbs at my core at the prospect of a few more hours with him. I'm not sure how much more my body can handle of him, but I'm willing to test the limits. His hand travels down my body as my legs involuntarily spread open for him. He's right...there's no reason to get out of bed.

I have no idea how I'll be able to walk away from this man today. I have no idea how I'll be able to walk *period*. What have I done? How was I supposed to know this guy would wreck me with orgasms and tender caresses? This is just physical. I need to keep reminding myself that the look in his eyes, and those tender touches, are pure physical lust. It isn't possible that this is a real connection we're having because we're complete strangers. A stranger who's working my body like he's known it all his life. He is no doubt a skilled lover. The multiple orgasms proved that point clearly. I'm getting attached faster to him than I have any other guy, which is the one thing I wasn't supposed to do. Maybe it's because I'm trying so hard to not fall for a guy, that I'm falling when I shouldn't be. I know, this isn't real, it's all in my head.

His fingers play my body as the thunder continues to rumble, and as the pleasure builds, all my worries and concerns drift away. He's working me like a plane about to take off, pushing all the right buttons and checking off every checklist he has to complete me. My body shakes with the building, and my heart pounds in my ears so loudly I can't hear anything else. Jim slides on top of me as his weight presses me into the mattress. He eases inside of me, and I feel myself rising higher and higher. He's already worked me up so much that it's not going to take me long to fall over that blissful edge. I dig my nails into his shoulders, and he releases a low growl. The sound is so erotic, so hot, that I moan as he pushes deeper into me.

My stomach tightens, and I wonder if I'm going to break in half, my body is wound so tight. Jim shifts his hips, the angle changing, and my question is unanswered—I break. I come undone in the most unreal and blissful way. I sigh into Jim's mouth and he groans as I feel his body tighten and then quiver.

This isn't genuine. It can't be. It's only physical. I try to remind myself over and over so I don't fall completely, so far I've only stumbled. So I tell myself over and over again the only thing that I can...

ARROGANT ARRIVAL

Jolene, tonight all this goes away...

Jimmy

I'm not ready to leave Jolene. I want to ask her for her phone number or for any way to contact her, but I'm terrified that this didn't mean the same to her as it did to me. It's crazy, but we have something. I just don't know if she realizes it or even wants it. After having her in the bed and again in our extra steamy shower, we both receive notifications that our flights are scheduled to leave tonight. We have to get back to the airport, and then we'll go our separate ways.

My phone rings again. I've been ignoring all my calls and messages, but this is a call from the private company I work for so I have to take it. Jolene is in the bathroom fixing her hair, so I hurry to answer.

"Hello, Jim here."

"Jim, we need you to take a flight tomorrow morning."

"Where to?"

"One of our executives needs to be in New Orleans by nine A.M. Then, they need to be back here by noon."

"That shouldn't be a problem."

"Can you do another flight tomorrow?"

"Most likely. What do you need?"

"This one is personal. My son has a game in Oxford. I need to leave after work."

"You got it." I remember him telling me his son plays college football.

"Thanks, I appreciate it."

"No problem. I'll keep an eye on the weather."

I end the call and find Jolene standing behind me. Shit, I quickly go over the phone conversation trying to think if I said anything flight related. I wave my phone and offer a sheepish smile. "Work. I'll use the restroom real quick and we should be good to go."

I sit my phone on the table and hurry off to the restroom before she can ask me again what it is I do for work. Even though I most likely won't ever see her again, I still would rather she didn't know I'm a pilot.

Jolene

Smiling as Jim walks to the restroom, I can't help but feel giddy and sad at the same time. I really like Jim. He's so playful, fun, and sweet. A little cocky, well, actually, a lot cocky, but it's part of his charm. Plus, that cockiness definitely comes with a guarantee in the bedroom. At least he's not a pilot. I can't believe the first guy I sleep with who's not a pilot could be someone I share a potential future relationship. Just goes to show I was right all along, I just need to avoid pilots. I'm not sure what I'm feeling right now, though. Sad, maybe, because I'm not ready to lose him. Maybe we could keep in touch and this all works out? Why not? I'm terrified of getting my heart broken, but I know it'll break the moment we part ways without exchanging numbers. Then I'll know I've lost him for good. At least this way, there might be a chance of something more, as crazy as that sounds.

ARROGANT ARRIVAL

Jim's phone lights up with an incoming text. I shouldn't even bother, it's not my place to take him his phone and he'll be out any moment. But he said he'd just gotten off with a work call. This might be important. I pick up the phone to quickly take it to him, but stop when I glance down.

DEX: Need a flight, man. Is your schedule clear for next Tuesday? I just had something come up and need to go to FL to visit my dad. Think you can fly me?

Why is someone asking Jim if he can fly them? I feel the palpations in my chest and a feeling of dread forms in the pit of my stomach. What have I done? Did this entire encounter begin as a lie? I told him I didn't want to get involved with a pilot again. I specifically told him no pilots.

I hear the sink turn off and quickly place the phone back down. Jim walks out smiling at me. "Ready."

"Jim?" I try to keep my voice calm.

"Yeah?"

"I think we can both agree that we had an incredible night–"

He comes to me and wraps his hands around my back. "Hell yeah, we did. I'm glad you enjoyed it as much as I did. It's a relief to hear you say that because I was hoping we could possibly see where this goes?"

I ease out of his grip so I can look into his eyes. "Possibly. I want to get to know you better, and see where do we go from here and is there an opportunity for us to reconnect in the future? Also, you know that

47

my job allows me to be in multiple cities and countries throughout any given week. But what does Jim the Greek do for a living? And would your job allow our paths to cross as easily in the future?"

He falters and then smiles, "How about Jimmy the Great? Or I guess I could be Jimmy the Greek god of sexiness?"

"Sure, if that's what you need to feel better about yourself. But what I need to know is what does his greatness do for a living?"

I don't miss how his body stiffens, how his eyes shift to the side. "I'm self-employed."

"Doing what?" I grit out. I'm struggling to control my temper when he is clearly deflecting.

"Okay. Listen, and hear me out before you get upset." He places his hands on my shoulders.

I can't believe this! I can't believe he lied to me! I fell for it again! I jerk out of his touch and shove him away. "You lied to me!"

"I haven't even said anything... How do you know I lied?"

"You're a pilot, aren't you?"

"How'd you know?"

"Your phone buzzed. I was worried it was important since you said you'd just gotten off a work call and started to bring it to you."

"So you read it along the way?"

"I glanced at it. I didn't swipe the screen or anything. But you knew I vowed not to sleep with another pilot and still...you bastard, was it a challenge for you then? A game? Did you get a good laugh, Jim?" I'm seething with rage. I want to slap him. I want to throw things. Most of all, I just want away from him.

ARROGANT ARRIVAL

"Absolutely not! It's not like that, Jo!" he shouts.

"Don't call me Jo! We're not friends! We're *nothing*!" Jim walks toward me with his arms out. I hold a hand up. "Don't you dare touch me." I speak through gritted teeth.

"So you're going to throw away last night and this morning over what I do for a living? That's discriminating and judgmental. And you are making assumptions about me that aren't true at all."

"Really?" I turn in a circle trying to rein in my rage. I place my hands on my hips and face him. I can hear the venom in my voice. "Not true at all, huh? This might've gone differently if you'd been honest up front. I'm not discriminating that you're a pilot. It's that you lied to me. Now I don't know what to believe. What part of any of it was real...was any of it the truth? Have you been honest with me at all?" Before he can speak, I hold a hand up. "Don't. Just don't. Save your words."

I go to walk past him and he grabs my hand and places it over his chest. I feel his heart beating. "Don't listen to my words then. What about this? What do you feel? Is that a lie?"

His heart is beating hard against his chest. "Trying to prove you have heart? You know what you've proven? Every man with a pulse lies." I jerk my hand free and turn to get the hell out of here. I don't know what to feel anymore. All I know is that despite promising myself I'd keep my heart safe, I let myself down yet again. I grab my carry on and hurry to the elevator and wait until the door closes to allow myself to cry for the last time over a man.

CHAPTER 5

Jolene

Dear Journal,

I did it again. I told myself I wouldn't, but here I am. Making a complete fool of myself. I'm so damn weak. Not only did I have a crappy flight where I was propositioned by a man to have a three-way with his wife, but my connecting flight gets canceled, so I go out and sleep with the first pilot I find. Just great. That was yesterday. Today, I won't worry about yesterday. Today is going to be awesome because I have an international flight to...wait for it... Paris, France. The city of love. However, I'm not looking for love in a man. I am going for coffee and macaroons. I will tour the Louvre and get lost in a world of beauty, forgetting my ugly past for a few days.

ARROGANT ARRIVAL

I close my journal and board the plane with Lana and Renee. We are back together to work this leg to Paris. Of course, they want all the amazing and awful details about Jim.

"You're kidding?" Lana asks.

"I wish I was! He was a pilot this whole time and he *knew* how I felt about men in that profession."

"But didn't say a word," Renee snarls as she shakes her head.

"Not a word," I confirm.

"Well, screw him," Lana says.

"She already did, and it was apparently amazing," Renee snickers, but then sees my glare. "Sorry."

I shove my luggage in the overhead bin as I make my way to the cockpit to introduce myself to the pilot and co-pilot working this flight. Next, I go through my pre-flight safety check of the emergency equipment, oxygen bottles, fire extinguisher, and finally get my flight safety demonstration items ready. I check on my phone for this flights' passenger count, and it looks like a full flight. Thankful for that, as a full flight means I stay busy and keep my mind off of Jim the Lying Greek god.

The passengers begin to come aboard. I smile and help people stow their luggage. Once our flight is taxiing, I go through the safety instructions. When I've finished that, I go through one more time to make sure everyone has everything stowed away and their chairs are in the correct position for takeoff.

I stop short when I spot a gentleman turned to the aisle with his socks and shoes off. I look around to see if anyone else is seeing this. The man is sitting there and clipping his toenails in the aisle.

This is going to be a long flight...

Dear Journal,

Paris is everything. The city is very clean and absolutely lovely. I didn't spend much time sight-seeing since I spent HOURS in the Louvre museum. I still didn't see everything, and I have no idea how I'll manage to work my flight tomorrow because my feet are killing me. The Egyptian section is beyond fascinating, and I think it was my personal favorite. Although, in the Denon wing, the statue Psyche Revived by Cupid's Kiss was by far my favorite piece of history in the entire museum. There was something so romantic and intimate about the pose. My eyes and heart were captivated by the piece. Of course, I did see the most famous piece of art, the Mona Lisa. It was much smaller than I expected. But I've read where other people have said the same thing. At sunset I took a walk along Ile de la Cite. There I saw the Notre Dame, and it is breathtakingly beautiful. There simply wasn't enough time for me on this layover. I hope to one day return to this stunning city of love.

ARROGANT ARRIVAL

Jimmy

After Jolene left, I was hurt and angry with myself. But now, sitting here in the night club, I'm angry with her. I'm frustrated that she didn't give me a chance, *us* a chance. She just stormed out of the hotel room—and my life—without even letting me explain myself. It's not like I told her I *wasn't* a pilot. It's not like I said I was a chef or car salesman. I never got a chance to say what I did for a living. *Okay, I did get a chance.* I'll give her that. I should've been honest up front, but I was scared. I wanted her so bad, and that's wrong too. I'm man enough to admit I fucked up, but she did too. She couldn't let me speak for five minutes to apologize and tell her I omitted the fact that I'm a pilot out of fear she'd reject me immediately. I wanted a chance to at least show her what we could have. I guess I only showed her that I'm like every other douche she's come across. Damn it. It's been two days, and I'm still thinking about her. This wasn't supposed to happen. I wish now it'd never stormed, and my flight hadn't been canceled. At least I can find comfort in that we won't ever cross paths again. If I'm lucky, anyway.

I might've dodged a bullet. I will go on being a carefree bachelor flying around the world and meeting beautiful women to spend my nights with. Beautiful women who don't have some crazy aversion to pilots. No, I'll be with women who love the fact I'm a pilot. I can take them to new heights in both the bedroom and outside the bedroom. I silently nod to myself and take a shot. *That's right, motherfuckers, I'm back in action.*

I eye the dancing bodies through the bright, multicolored strobe lights. I'm in Los Angeles tonight because my boss had a meeting. That's one flight I never turn down. Layovers in L.A. are the best. I spot a stunning, curvy blond. I definitely don't want any brunettes for a while. *Not that they remind me of anyone or anything.* I watch her until she makes eye contact with me. She smiles and nods. *Green light.*

I stand up from the bar stool and make my way through the bodies to her. I lean toward her and speak over the music in her ear. "I'm sorry that I was staring. I couldn't seem to take my eyes off you."

"Why look when you can touch?" She takes my hands and places them on her swaying hips. *No bullshitting around. I like her.*

We dance a little, and then I ask her if she'd like a drink. She nods, and I guide her to the bar. She leans toward me and says over the music. "Are you a local?"

"No. Just here for the night."

"What brings you to L.A.?"

"My work. I'm a pilot." *Let's get that out there and in her face before we go any further.*

A huge smile stretches across her face. "No shit? Which airline? I'm a flight attendant."

Oh, fuck me, not again. "I'm sorry. I have to go." I drop some cash on the bar for both our drinks and leave like my ass is on fire.

CHAPTER 6

Jimmy – One month later...

I silently groan as my mother hounds me again about providing her with grandchildren and will she live to be a yia-yia. The woman isn't even fifty, but acts like her final days are just around the corner. I'm still in my twenties, so I feel like we all have plenty of time before our clocks start ticking, but try to tell that to a Greek mother. She wants grandkids and she wants them now.

"Jimmy Mou..." My mother's heavy Greek accent calls to me saying *My Jimmy*. It comes off lovingly, yet scolding me at the same time. *A skill only she has mastered.*

She called to see how my flight went to Chicago, but somehow it's come back around to when am I going to start a family. "What about your yia-yia? Huh? Do you not care? She wants to be able to see you at your wedding. But *no*. All you do is fly around in the sky, free as a bird. But you know what else birds do? They build nests. They build nests for their families. When are you going to build a nest and start a family, Dimitrios?"

Bringing my grandma into this conversation is a low blow from Ma. She knows how much I love that feisty old bird. I know they all want to see me settle down and have children, preferably get married to a nice Greek girl with a huge Greek wedding and procreate Greek babies, at least one boy to carry the family name, but this bird is still spreading his wings.

"You know, my cousin Maria said she knows of a—"

"Oh, I'm sorry, Ma, but I have an incoming call from my client. I've got to go. He's probably finished his meeting and needs me to fly him back home."

"Alright, Jimmy. You come back home and we can discuss over dinner, yeah?"

I don't want to discuss her playing the Greek matchmaker, but I also hate to miss out on her cooking. Decisions, decisions, decisions.

"I'll be there by five."

"Bravo, Jimmy! Be safe. S'agapo para polli androuli mou!"

I tell her that I love her too and end the call. There's got to be some way to get them to let this go. My Ma and Yia-Yia are stubborn women, though. They're not going to be satisfied until I'm married and off producing many little Greeklings. My phone rings again and I see it's my cousin Bianca.

"Don't tell me Ma has already called you," I groan into the phone.

She giggles. "No. Why would she?"

"Oh, I just figured she sent you on a mission to scour New York to find me a Greek bride."

"I mean, she's asked me to before, but not today. Well, not yet anyway, it's still early." I can hear the smile in her voice.

ARROGANT ARRIVAL

"That's not surprising. You better be glad that your parents were so laid back. They didn't care whether or not you and Dex got married right away, or whether or not he was Greek."

"We had other issues to worry about, if you recall. Like whether or not he was my step-brother."

"Yeah, well, I think Ma's *only* requirement is that I marry a Greek. Not too sure if she's worried about whether or not we're related."

"Ew! Jimmy, no. Thea isn't that bad." Thea is the Greek word for aunt. We both laugh, even though I'm only halfway joking, and she is too. "I wanted to call you about a trip."

"Sure. Need me to fly you somewhere or just transport a plane?"

"Actually, I wanted you on the plane with me. I've never been to Greece. You've gotten to meet our family over there, and now that I have my own family... I don't know. I just really want to meet them and thought we could take a family vacation. Would you go with us?"

"As long as it's me introducing you to family, and nobody trying introduce me to available bachelorettes. Absolutely no one is allowed to try and marry me off while we're there." "I can't make any promises for anybody else, but you're safe with me and Dex. I don't think little Georgina will try to marry you off either."

This won't be much of a vacation if I have everyone hounding me. If my mother could, she'd have me married while we're there. But, honestly, I haven't been to Greece in three years, so it would be nice to visit everyone again. "I don't have any flights scheduled the beginning of next month. I'll keep that week cleared. Sound good?"

"Perfect. Might even extend it to, say, nine days? I'll see if Dex and I can clear our schedule as well."

"Give Georgina kisses for me."

"Will do! Bye, Jimmy."

I end the call and sigh. Taking a commercial flight to Greece makes me automatically think of Jo. I hate it that my mind keeps going back to her. Anything and everything reminds me of her. I haven't even eaten cheesecake again. I wonder what my pilot-hating stewardess has been up to. I wonder if I'll ever see her again. Despite knowing it's ridiculous, I can't stop thinking about her. It's been a month, and I'm still hung up over her. There was something about her that has me regretting not getting her full name or phone number before she stormed off, pissed. All because of what? That I'm a pilot? She's the ridiculous one. She's so ridiculous that she's made me ridiculous. She's an airline stewardess who hates pilots. That's like an actor who hates cameramen.

The executive that I'm flying walks through the door right then, interrupting me from my thoughts. "Thank you for waiting on me, Jimmy."

"No problem, sir. Ready to head out?"

"Yes. I hope you weren't too bored while waiting?"

Pining over a woman I barely know and can't find, listening to my meddling mother trying to marry me off to the first available Greek woman who comes along, and planning a vacation in Greece with my cousin and her wealthy husband? Nope. Not bored at all. The only silver lining is I'll get to play with my sweet niece Georgina on some of the most beautiful beaches in the world.

CHAPTER 7

Jolene

It's been two months since my epic night of passion, but dammit if I can't stop thinking about him. Worse, if I hear anything Greek, it reminds me of him, that and Elvis Presley. An Elvis song was playing in the Memphis International Airport, for obvious reasons, so I had to plug in my headphones. The bright side is that I'm completely over all the other heartaches and crushes. In fact, I'm so over any guy who's not Jim that I don't even give anyone a second glance. If I close my eyes, I can still feel and hear him. It's great for a few minutes, my memories tiding me over until I open them and see that I'm still alone.

I sigh and look out the window of the plane. All these adventures I go on, and my most incredible night was a rainy layover in Miami with a stranger. The captain comes over the intercom and tells us to prepare for landing. Lana sits across from me and smiles. She has that look like she's about to share a naughty secret.

"What did you do?" I drawl out.

"It's not what I did, but who I'm hoping to do."

I laugh and shake my head at her. "Okay...who's the lucky guy?"

Lana grins. "George."

"The new co-pilot?" I point my finger behind me.

"Yes. Isn't he dreamy?"

I hadn't really noticed. *I haven't noticed anyone since...* I force a smile. "Well, way to welcome him to the team."

"I'm nice like that. But there's a slight problem that you could easily fix, my dearest and bestest friend and coworker." I roll my eyes and she reaches across, grabbing my hands. "You have a layover in New York tonight and so does George. I have a leg to Athens. But since you don't want to hook-up with George—him being a bad ol' pilot and all, I could do this for you and let you have my connecting flight to Greece?"

Jim. Great. Even Greece is ruined for me. I'm so annoyed at myself for immediately thinking of Jim when Lana asks me to cover her shift to Athens, Greece. I've never been to Greece, so the thought is exciting and I could stay there a bit longer to take in the sights since I don't have to work for a few days. I'm not sure if it's the plane descending, or just my thoughts of Jim, but it causes my chest to sting and tighten. We bounce a little as the wheels hit the runway. Lana bats her long eyelashes at me and I cave. "Fine. But don't think I noticed how you tried to make this sound as though you're doing me a favor when it's you who will be smiling by the end of the night."

Lana just laughs because she knew what she was doing. That traitor.

ARROGANT ARRIVAL

We land and wish the passengers a wonderful stay and tell them we hope that they will fly with us again. The normal spiel. Once the plane is empty, I turn to Lana, "I guess I'll let you handle clean-up since I need to rush and catch my next flight to Greece." Lana sticks her tongue out at me as George appears in the doorway of the cockpit. She quickly slips it back in her mouth and smiles at him. *Good luck, George, you're gonna need it with this one.*

Why can't I be more Lana and Renee? They don't have any issue having fun and being spontaneous with these pilots. Why do I keep letting myself get attached? Worse, I realize I just thought I was hung up on the guys before. That was a crush. Jim has gone past crushing me but ruining me. I don't even want to think about hooking up with not only pilots, but anyone, for that matter.

When I board the plane, none other than Captain Clynes, aka Trip, greets me. I should be happy for him, and in a way, I am. I'm surprised to see that *Mrs.* Clynes and baby Brucey is on board the plane as well. I shouldn't be too surprised. Sometimes they do travel with him. It must be so romantic and nice to fly and see the world together. That's everything that I thought I could have.

"Hello, Kendall."

"Hey, Jolene." She smiles.

I look down at the adorable baby boy, "Hello," I coo. My heart tightens, and I force myself to smile. I quickly go to work so we can take off on time. As the passengers board, my back is turned toward the back of the plane when I swear I hear his voice. *No. That can't be him.* Sure enough, I turn around and there's Jim—*with a child!* I stare in horror at the beautiful, dark-haired little girl in his arms. He's speaking to Trip while a stunning dark-haired woman stands next to him, smiling lovingly at the little girl. No doubt she's the mother. My blood is boiling, and I can hear my heart pounding in my ears. I'm going to be trapped on a ten-hour flight with Jim and his *family*. This is some horrible twist of fate or punishment. I'm not sure which one yet. I wasn't even supposed to be on this flight. This is punishment for submitting poor George to Lana, I just know it.

"Jolene!" One of my co-workers calls out. *Shoot!* Immediately, Jim's eyes widen as they scan the plane. To my surprise, he smiles widely when our eyes meet. He shakes Trip's hand and then walks toward me. *What is he doing? Is he seriously planning to rub it in my face that he has a family? He has a family—oh my gosh. That's a new low for me. I slept with a married man. A man who's married with a child!*

Too many travelers are in his way, so it takes a moment for him to get through. He is persistent, I'll give him that. He waves and gives me a small smile. "Jolene."

For a moment, I debate over pretending I don't know him. How would his inflated ego like that? Freaking jerk. Instead, I force a smile since there are passengers and a sweet child now between us. "Hello... Jim."

"How have you been?" His eyes are asking so much more. Those blue green eyes shine bright as they search mine. He has a little more dark facial stubble.

ARROGANT ARRIVAL

His black hair is a little longer on top and messy. He's also wearing a black leather jacket, white button up and dark denim jeans. And damn does he wear that outfit well. The little girl in his arm is a nice accessory. She's absolutely adorable. "Jo?"

Him saying my nickname brings me out of my thoughts. *Why, that arrogant... What right does he have using my nickname?* I put a smile on my face since we have an audience. He must mistake my smile for happiness, or he just wants to further irritate me, because he continues talking like everything is hunky dory. "The stars have aligned, and fate has brought us together yet once again."

"Yes. Only this time with your family." I swallow the lump in my throat and maintain my smile, even though my heart is shattering. The mention of family has him smiling with...*pride*. I just don't understand how he can be grinning right now.

"Right? I'd like for you to meet my princess, Georgina." He hoists the beautiful little girl up higher and beams at her. She smiles at me and offers a shy little wave.

"Hello, precious." I give her a genuine smile, because despite her father being a cad, she is absolutely a doll. I decide to tell her as much, just in case any of my bitchy vibes are radiating. "You're absolutely precious." I lean toward Jim and grumble, "Despite who her father is."

Jim laughs and nods his head in agreement. "Ha. I didn't realize you knew Dex. I guess most people do know him. It is hard to believe such a little sweetheart–"

"Dex? She's not yours?"

His eyebrows pull together. "She's mine..." He holds her tighter, that bastard...the smirk that spreads across his face. He better be glad he's holding that little girl to his face. "My *niece*." The little girl begins to fidget. "You ready for mama?"

The stunning brunette who had boarded the plane with him comes toward us. "Come here, sweetheart. Is Theo trying to use you to flirt with the pretty lady? He's such a tool." I smile, immediately liking this woman. She smiles back at me as she takes her daughter and carries her away toward the front of the plane to first class.

"Theo?" I ask.

"That's the word for uncle in Greek." He looks around and then takes a step closer to me. Placing his face close to mine, he whispers, "You know, if I didn't know any better I'd think you were jealous when you thought—"

"Jealous, more like livid since I thought you were a lying cheater, and not just a liar. You know nothing." I step back and force my voice to sound professional, "Now, if you'll please take your seat, sir."

"Oh, is that how you want to play it?"

I try to school my facial expressions and stand tall. I'm a professional, and I'd deal with him as I would any other passenger. "Sir, we need to get the plane loaded. Please take your seat."

Instead, he takes a step toward me and whispers, "Not until I get one thing cleared up. I'm not involved with anyone, and I haven't slept with anyone since you. You kind of ruined me for anyone else, if you must know. I can still smell you, taste you, still want you. And just to clarify, I have family, a lot of nosey, obnoxious family, but no wife and kids."

I swallow hard and feel my knees about to buckle under his intense blue gaze. Attempting to take back some of my dignity, I respond, "I didn't think about you at all."

He grins and takes a step back. "It's okay. You don't have to admit it." He turns his back on me and calls out, "You were always on my mind." With that, he walks toward first class.

He actually quoted another Elvis song. That asshole.

Jimmy

I hum the hit song, "You Were Always on My Mind," while I sit in my seat in first class. *Fate is smiling down on me. What are the odds that we'd be on the same flight to Greece together?*

"I thought I should let you know, since you are committed to this flight now, Thea has already informed the family in Greece that you're coming to find a bride."

I almost jump out of my seat. I couldn't have heard Bianca correctly. "What? No, no, no. Ma promised me she would not play matchmaker. I told her it was the only way I'd go with you guys."

"She's not. She didn't lie to you. The *rest* of the country is going to do it for her."

I groan. I guess we know where I get my twisting of words and omitting the truth from. I try to figure out a way to enjoy my summer without having to deal with all the women in my life trying to marry me off.

Bianca shrugs and whispers. "A woman named Pamela is apparently the front runner so far, but I hear there's other contenders."

"Hell no to Pamela."

"You know her?"

"Yes. She's a royal bitch. At one time when I was younger I thought she was hot, but as soon as I got to know her, I started thinking with the right brain. No. Just no."

"Hello. Anything I can get you to drink?" I look up into the flight attendant's blue eyes, wishing they were Jolene's brown eyes. For such an enclosed space, she sure has managed to avoid me.

Dex and Bianca give their orders while I scan for my sexy stewardess. When I spot her, an idea forms. A rather brilliant idea. Jolene could easily pass for a Greek woman. She could be my girlfriend for the trip, and then go back to hating me. Let's be honest, there's not much difference between love and hate, is there?

"Excuse me," I leap from my chair and hurry toward the other section of the plane where I had spotted Jolene with her drink cart.

"I need to speak with you."

"I'm busy, Jim," she growls through her teeth.

"It's important."

"Sir, please, take your seat and I'll have the first-class stewardess come to you in a moment."

"I can't take a seat, and I don't want or need the other stewardess. I have to get this off my chest. Now."

ARROGANT ARRIVAL

Jolene's eyes widen as her smile remains plastered on her face, "Okay. Let me finish here and I'll be right with you."

I grin to the two elderly ladies who are in their seat waiting for their drink. Jolene hands one of the women her club soda. As she takes it, she blushes and says to me, "I wouldn't keep you waiting, hot stuff."

"Ummm, I appreciate that." I give her a full smile and then turn to Jolene and wink before I turn around to go back to my seat.

My leg nervously bounces while I wait for Jolene. Bianca turns to look at me and frowns. "Are you okay? I didn't peg you to be a nervous flyer, considering your profession."

I chuckle and shake my head. "Don't be ridiculous."

"Is it Thea and Yia-Yia? You still have a couple of hours before you have to deal with them. At least they're not seated with us." She nudges me with her elbow. "You're welcome."

"Couple of more hours," I mumble to myself.

CHAPTER 8

Jolene

What the hell could Jim possibly need that's an emergency? My stomach flips the closer I get to him. I plaster a smile on my face and in my most professional voice, say, "Sir, can I get you anything?"

Jim's eyes widen, and he quickly looks at the woman sitting next to him holding the little girl. He turns back to me and whispers. "Let's go somewhere more private?"

His cousin must've heard because she hisses. "You're on a plane, Jimmy. Where do you think you're going to go that's private? The cargo hold?" I see the exact moment her mind wanders to the wrong idea. Her eyes widen in horror and her jaw drops. "You better not, Jimmy Georgakopolous!" The other gentleman with them snickers.

Jim rolls his eyes. "Not for that. Have you seen the size of lavatories on planes?" He stands and I follow him toward the back of the plane to where we keep our supplies. Two of my co-workers are standing back

ARROGANT ARRIVAL

there, so Jim and I stand there awkwardly until they take the hint and walk away. I cross my arms and wait expectantly for him to tell me what it is he needed to speak to me so badly about.

"Fancy meeting you here. How ya been?" His playful smile gives him such a boyish charm...but I'm not falling for it again.

"Really? Cut to the chase. What is it?"

"Right." Jim claps his hands and swallows. "I need you."

I can't deny that my heart skips a beat and I feel myself getting warm in all the right places just from his raspy voice saying those words to me.

Jim takes a step closer. "Stay in Greece with me. Spend nine days with me there..." he searches my eyes "...as my girlfriend."

"Your girlfriend? Surely you're joking. What part of me saying I wouldn't date a pilot again did you not comprehend?" Is he serious about wanting to have a relationship? I want to scream right now. "Why now? Because you saw me and decided you needed a little extra fun while there?"

"Well, I saw you and decided I needed you to be my girlfriend. My Greek girlfriend, to be exact."

"What? Go sit back down now, you asshole." Did he just ask me to be his Greek girlfriend? Hellllooo, I'm not even one-tenth Greek. This is beginning to sound like he just wants to use me as a prop, and I'm not buying what he's selling.

"Jo...hear me out." Jim comes closer and places his hands on my shoulders. "My Ma and Yia-Yia—"

"You're what?"

"My mother and grandmother. Anyway, please listen to what I'm asking of you." I nod and he continues, "Those crazy Greek women are determined to try and get me to settle down. They're also very Greek and... would love for me to marry a Greek girl and have little Greek babies. However, if I have a girlfriend with me... it would make them pairing me with someone in the Mother Land very difficult."

"That all sounds horrible and completely inopportune for you, but I'm afraid I won't be of any help for a variety of reasons. See, I'm not Greek. And you lied to me, so I don't like you. Plus, I don't date pilots, remember?"

"But you look Greek. Not all Greek Americans speak Greek. Bianca doesn't. You don't have to like me. And about the pilot thing, we wouldn't actually be dating, just pretending."

I don't know why it stings that he's only asking for me to be his *pretend* girlfriend. Why can't he just want me to go because he's missed me? Has he missed me? I know it was supposed to be a one-night stand and I know I left things between us in a very heated way, but after what we shared...

"You want to use me?" I cross my arms.

"Only for a little while."

"Are you kidding me right now?"

"That came out wrong." Jim holds his hands up.

I think back to the woman who is sitting next to him. "The guy sitting with you. Is he Greek?"

"Dex? No. Bianca's parents are more open than mine. I mean, they even got a divorce. My father only got away from my mother because he passed away by what we're assuming were natural causes." The way he

ARROGANT ARRIVAL

says it has me more nervous to meet his mother. What does he mean they assume he died of natural causes? That little tidbit scares me more than the potential of being around this man for nine days. "My family is very traditional Greek. Whereas Bianca's is more American Greek. My family in Greece are..." he sighs, "...they believe in older values. They hold on to the culture, traditions, and are old fashioned."

"Is your Ma going to be there?"

"Yeah, yeah. She's here on the plane with my Yia-Yia." Jim waves his hand as though that's not important, but clearly it is since this woman is the one who has him trying to con me into being his fake girlfriend.

"They're on the plane?"

"Yeah."

"Think they're not going to notice? How you magically pop up with a girlfriend? Come on." I start to walk away, but Jim steps in front of me.

"I plan on surprising them with the news. Anyway, Ma has been on me about marrying a Greek and continuing Greek traditions for as long as I can remember. I don't want to bore you with all that. In fact, I don't want to bore you at all. We can have a *very* exciting time in Greece. I can show you all the beautiful sights that regular tourists don't get to experience." Jim takes a loose strand of my hair and twirls it around his finger. "Drinking coffee on the beach, dancing into the morning hours, and eating some of the best food you'll ever have in your life. Doesn't sound too bad, does it?"

No, actually it sounds kind of nice. "I'll need to think about it. I have a job. I can't take a full week off. I was going to stay a couple of days on my own, but nine days?"

"Sure, you can. Just don't get back on the plane..." When I scowl at him, he holds his hands up. "I'm kidding. Have someone cover your shifts." I roll my eyes and start to step around him. He hurries to say, "I'll pay for all of your expenses and ticket back. Seven days, full expenses paid in one of the top destinations in the world. All you have to do is to pretend to be in love with me. Come on. What do you have to lose?" *What's left of my heart. That's all.* "I'll have to think about it."

"Great, you have nine hours. That should be enough time, right?"

Wrong. I only needed nine seconds to know there's no way I'm spending nine days with him and his crazy family.

While all the passengers drift off to sleep, I can't help but think about his offer. Seven days as Jim's girlfriend. Correction—his pretend girlfriend. I haven't been in a fully committed relationship to even know how to pretend. Not only do I have to pretend to be his girlfriend, but his *Greek* girlfriend. It's so absurd. I plan to avoid him for the rest of this flight, when we land, and hopefully, the rest of my life.

As Jim walks by to exit the plane, Trip pats his shoulder and shakes his hand again. "Thanks for the info, man. I'll definitely look into it."

Jim smiles broadly. "Yeah, you should. I love being a contract pilot. You get to do what you love, but on your own schedule." He leans toward Trip. "It's great. Especially for a family man." He smiles at Kendall and then exits the plane.

ARROGANT ARRIVAL

A family. I turn to look at Kendall holding their son while smiling at Trip. So much love between those two. I try to swallow the lump in my throat and ignore the ache in my heart. Once all the passengers have left the plane, everyone discusses what they're going to do for our layover, and just then, something inside of me clicks.

"What about you, Jolene?"

I look over my shoulder from picking up some trash left in a seat. All eyes are on me. Not wanting to admit that I have no plans, or anyone to spend this time with, I straighten my back and smile. "I'm actually spending some time here in Greece."

"How long?"

"I'm spending nine days with a friend and their family." I blush and give a small smile.

"Wow!" I can't help but like how, for once, people are envious of me and that I have a life outside of work. *Now I need to rush off and find him before my vacation in Greece is nothing more than a myth.*

CHAPTER 9

Jolene

My nerves are a mess as I quickly scan the baggage claim for Jim. *Shit, what if I missed him?* "Looking for someone?"

I jump at the low voice in my ear from behind. Spinning around, I come face to face with Jim's cat-that-swallowed-the-canary smirk. "No." *Not anymore.*

Of course, it's clear that Jim can see right through my lie the way he keeps smiling. He's so damn arrogant. "Search no more, gorgeous, your Greek lover has arrived."

"I'm already starting to regret this."

"I don't think you're going to regret having me whenever you want for nine days straight. In fact, you may not know how to live without me once this is over."

"*Wow*. Your ego is…I don't even have words."

"Don't worry. It's not the first time I've made you speechless, and it won't be the last."

Jim's phone buzzes. He swipes the screen, "Hello? No, I didn't run off. Bianca, I'm coming right now. I'm

ARROGANT ARRIVAL

coming. Yeah. Has Ma and Yia-Yia gotten their luggage? Okay. We're coming. Yes, *we*." His eyes brighten as he smiles at me. His voice drips with mischief. "You'll see," he says into the phone.

Ending the call, he wraps an arm around me. "Now you won't even have to act when convincing everyone you're in love with me...but we do need to be on the same page about when our relationship began. I say we just stick to the truth, we met on a layover two months ago and had an instant connection."

"Won't it look suspicious you never told them I was joining you?"

"It's a surprise. You weren't sure you could get off work until the last minute. And I didn't want my family harassing you while you worked."

"Speaking of," I open my phone to go to our online schedule. I check to see who's working and around the area to trade shifts with. I quickly shoot some messages to get shifts swapped.

"By the way, what's your last name?"

"All this time and you don't know my last name? What kind of shoddy boyfriend are you?"

Jim shrugs. "You never told me."

"It's Tanner."

"Now it's Tannerelos. You're Greek-American."

Tannerelos? Nobody is going to buy that. This is going to be all one big lie after another. Over a week of lying to his family and of us pretending to be committed to one another. God, we're both going to hell. Jim must notice me second-guessing myself because he wraps his arms around me again.

"Think about it, you will be saving me and some other poor woman from being shoved in each other's faces. Everyone will be able to enjoy their vacation because they won't be worrying about me being a bachelor forever. Even though, that's the plan."

"You really don't mind lying, do you? Don't answer that. So, you don't think you'll ever settle down?"

"Not you, too..." He sighs. "I'm sure I will eventually, but right now I like traveling the world and having my freedom. There's time. This isn't like when my grandparents and parents were growing up. People are living longer and people have options and careers. I've got time."

"But do you want to be an old man when your child wants to play baseball?"

"Soccer. My child will play soccer. We're Greek." He holds me tighter to his firm body. "And I'll show you old man. Just wait until we get to the house..."

I break free from his hold and smirk. "Who said you were getting those perks on this trip? You only said to *pretend* to be your girlfriend. So we can *pretend* to have sex while sleeping in separate beds."

"No, no. You're to be my *real girlfriend* for this trip. Only pretend you love me. Do I need to remind you about that amazing connection we shared? Would that help?" Jim gives me a lopsided smile and leans closer to me. "And I aim to be the best boyfriend you've ever had."

That shouldn't be hard to do. My history of boyfriends is nothing to brag about. Jim's phone buzzes again. He groans and hooks his arm over my shoulder. "We need to get to the others. They're growing impatient and ready to get home."

"Well, we did just get off a really long flight. They're exhausted."

ARROGANT ARRIVAL

"I hope you're not too exhausted." He winks.

Standing next to the door that leads outside the airport are Bianca, her husband whom I believe Jim said was Dex, their daughter Georgina, an older woman, and an elderly woman.

"Ma and Yia-Yia, your hunt for me to be with someone can end. Everyone, this is Jo! We met a couple of months ago, and now we're official. I'm bringing her to meet the family."

His mother's eyes go wide as she looks me up and down. She tilts her head and asks Bianca. "*Joe*? Did he say Joe?"

The grandmother pinches her pointer and middle fingers together to her thumb and makes the motion of a cross three times touching her forehead, shoulders, and chest. She begins mumbling some words in Greek.

Bianca shakes her head and rolls her eyes as the other woman studies me. She stops the elderly woman and I hear her whisper, "She's a woman, Yia-Yia."

"Jo-*lene*. Jo is a nickname," Jim emphasizes. He turns to me and gives me a sheepish smile. "Yia-Yia can't see very well and she thought I was calling you Joe, as in with an 'e.' And, anyway, let's get going." Jim lets out a nervous chuckle and I force a smile. *Well, this is already off to a great start.*

Jim clears his throat, "Jolene, you've sort of met my cousin Bianca, her husband Dex, and their daughter Georgina, whom you've already met. This stunning goddess here is my mother Martha and my grandmother Patty. Everyone Jolene Tannerelos."

I shake everyone's hand. I think I'm in the clear until Martha asks, "So...you're Greek?"

I nod, but before I can clarify I've never spoke Greek or know *anything* about Greece other than what I learned in a high school history class, Martha jumps into speaking Greek.

"Um, Ma, she doesn't speak Greek. She never learned the language. Like Bianca!"

Yia-Yia Patty begins mumbling in Greek again. I want to tell Jim that this idea of his may be hopeless and backfire because I don't think I'm scoring him any points. They'll be ready to replace me and work even harder now on finding him an honest-to-God Greek girl.

We walk over to the rental car service. Jim whispers to me, "Dex has already booked us two rental cars and a condo in Lefkada."

"That's where your family is from?"

"Sort of. My family is from a nearby village in Lefkada but we prefer to stay more in town. But *we* don't have to stay there the whole time. We could even go to a different island, just the two of us for a day or two."

"That would be amazing. But really, I'm excited just to explore any area of Greece."

"Believe me, after a couple of days with my *whole* family, you'll be ready to go exploring. You may even be ready to jump in the ocean and swim to another island."

"You know I hear you, adrouli mou. And I don't appreciate what you're telling this young woman. We are not that bad."

"Yes, not *that* bad." Jim mouths, "They *are*."

Dex hands Jim a set of keys. "Bianca, Georgina, and I will follow you."

ARROGANT ARRIVAL

I lean toward Jim and whisper, "I thought you said we're going to an island? Are we taking the cars with us and riding a ferry boat?"

"No. We're driving the whole way."

"I can't tell if you're being a smart ass or not."

"Lefkada is an island, but it's connected by a bridge so we can drive there, sweetheart. Get ready for the vacation of your life. Trust me."

Easier said than done since he's already lied to me once.

Jimmy

I'm driving the winding roads around the mountains of Greece with my Ma, Yia-Yia, and *Jolene—my fake Greek girlfriend*. It's not the strangest situation I've been in, if I'm being honest. Yia-Yia sits in the front passenger seat dressed in all black. She's worn only black since my Pappou passed away eight years earlier.

"Jimmy, agapi mou," *Jimmy, my love.*

"Nai, Yia-Yia," *Yes, Grandma.*

My Yia-Yia asks me questions on where I found 'this Jo', and what do I know about her and her family. In Greek, I tell her.

"Yia-Yia, she's a good girl. No, that's not a boy's name. You'll like her once you give her a chance. I've not met her family yet. Let's just enjoy our vacation."

She continues in Greek, "So you're not serious? You bring her all the way to meet all your family with no promises? Maybe she's not the one, then. Maybe this means you still need to meet the nice girl Maria knows."

"No, no, no. I think Jolene *is* the one."

"We'll see."

My mother, who has been watching Jolene out of the corner of her eye, leans forward, "Adrouli mou xruse." *My golden boy.* "It's good to meet people. What's meant to be will be, so what's the harm?"

"Ah! What's meant to be will be? So, you can leave well enough alone, then, too? Now I'd kindly ask you to only speak in English. We're being rude to Jo."

Ma lets out a huff and crosses her arms. Jolene remains quiet with her eyes fixed out the window. I look out to see what she's staring at and I'd almost forgotten how beautiful the country is. The mountains to one side and the deep blue Mediterranean Sea to the other. I notice her eyes look heavy. I turn up the radio and let my favorite Greek singer, Giannis Ploutarhos, fill our silence. I won't bother Jolene because I'm sure she's tired. We got to sleep on the flight over, she didn't. It'll be good for her to get some rest. Sure enough, the next time I look in the rearview mirror, her eyes are closed. I admire her beautiful cheek bones and notice she has a strong jawline as well. Her silky midnight hair has a few loose strands. I feel a sting on my arm and yelp.

"Eyes on the road, or you'll be looking at her in a coffin." I flinch at my yia-yia's harsh, yet valid, point.

"Did you pinch me?" I ask her in English.

She shrugs and goes back to looking out the window. I focus on the beauty before me. The mountains, the sea, and the vineyards as I drive the winding roads.

ARROGANT ARRIVAL

It's so damn good to be back in Greece.

It's late by the time we arrive at the condo, so we order takeout of gyros and souvlaki, and while we wait for our food to arrive, I join Jolene outside on the balcony. She's standing with her arms wrapped around herself, listening and watching the waves crash on to the beach.

"This is incredible," she whispers in awe.

"It is. I'd forgotten how beautiful Greece is. We used to visit almost every summer when my Pappou was still alive. He was the main one who wanted to come visit his sisters and cousins. After he died, we slowed down to every other summer. Then my father passed away from cancer."

"I'm sorry." She frowns. "Didn't you say you thought it was natural causes?"

"Well, my aunts believe it was from using the microwave too much. And somehow him using it too much was Ma's fault. So some of the family believes natural causes equals cancer and others say he was 'given' cancer."

Her mouth opens and closes a few times before she finally says, "Either way, I'm sorry."

"Thank you. Our last vacation with him was here in Greece. He wanted to see his home country one last time. It's been three years since I've been back. We still have a house up in the village. It's too small for all of us, though. That's where Pappou always wanted to go, up in the mountains. It's strange being back without him. I'm glad I have you here to be a distraction." I clear my throat. I'm not ready to get into any deep conversations tonight. "Dex rented this place for all of us, but by the way he's talking since we've arrived he may just buy a house in Greece."

"Would you want a house in Greece?"

I chuckle. "I should probably get a house in America first. Right now I'm renting a cheap place because I'm never home. Even when I'm not on a flight, I'm not home."

"Why?"

"What's the point of sitting in an empty house? It's boring and..."

"Lonely." Her voice holds sadness.

I swallow and nod in agreement. "Yeah, lonely," I whisper. I clap my hands and grin, "We won't get lonely here, that's for sure. We'll probably be missing our quiet places after a couple of days of this insanity."

As if on cue, my Ma yells out. "Jimmy mou! You and Hoelene come eat! Food's here!"

I cringe. "Sorry."

Jolene laughs. "It's not the first time I've been called that, but it is the first time with a Greek accent, so it has sort of a distinguished air to it."

We laugh and I take her hand. "Thank you, Jolene. I'm really glad you came."

"You know, *Dimitrios*...I am, too."

Let's hope you still are after seven days.

CHAPTER 10

Jolene

Dear Journal,

I'm spending nine days in Greece with none other than the lying asshole pilot whom I stupidly get butterflies every time I look at his arrogant face. Jim's mother Martha made it clear we'd sleep in separate beds, in separate rooms, since we're not married. Which was more than fine with me. It was the appropriate thing to do while in the same house with his mom and grandmother. However, if his Ma only knew what her precious golden boy had been doing with me two months ago in a bed...

I wake up to find my journal still open on my bed. I must've fallen asleep while writing. Turns out, all of us pretty much slept in to recover from the jet lag, and after eating a delicious meal of eggs, dry toast, and the strongest coffee ever, we are ready to go out and explore. It's almost noon, and I'm excited to walk down to the beach that I saw yesterday from the balcony. I knew my two-piece was a mistake when I walked by his grandmother and she made a cross again. Praying for my soul, as well as her grandson's, apparently. She kept using the word *kolo* as she hissed to Jim's mother. I have to remember to ask him what that means when we are alone.

I slip off my flipflops and toss my towel onto a beach chair. As I'm applying sunscreen, I look over to Jim who is holding his towel in front of his swim trunks. "What are you doing?"

"My Ma is on the balcony watching. I'm trying to calm myself down before I lay my towel down."

I look over to the balcony and then back to him. "W-o-w. You honestly think anyone will be able to see your erection from that far away? Please, I'm standing right here and it's not really that *noticeable*."

Jim chuckles and steps closer to me. "Sweetheart, I was worried about poking your eye out. I've calmed down now."

"Well, sorry I was the reason for your discomfort to start with. I guess I underestimated how you'd react seeing me in a swimsuit."

I watch as Jim removes his shirt, revealing his bronze skin and toned abs. I'd bite my tongue off before I'd admit how hot he looks right now. I quickly avert my eyes, but it's obvious the bastard caught me. "Feast your eyes. It's okay. And how do you know it was *you* who got me in this predicament? Thinking mighty highly of yourself."

I arch a brow and turn my back to him. I add a little sway to my hips as I make my way to the water and smile to myself when I hear him groan. *That's how I know.*

When Jim and I are out in the water and away from everyone, I ask, "What does *kolo* mean?"

Jim coughs and bursts out laughing. "It means butt. Where did you hear that?"

"Your yia-yia! She kept staring at me and saying it."

"Well, you do have a nice *kolo*." I hate the way my stomach flips when he says it with his Greek accent.

"I don't think she approves of my swimsuit."

He swims closer to me. "I think every man here, though, most assuredly approves of it. I'll admit that I do."

"Stop it. You know what I mean. I don't think she approves of me either. They are probably now gathering Greek women by the droves, and will have them waiting in the wings like a prison lineup. You might be wasting your time by having me here as your *pretend* girlfriend."

Jim swims closer toward me and begins to circle me like a shark. "Babe, there's worse ways to spend my time. Swimming in the Mediterranean with a gorgeous woman who has the most phenomenal kolo is not considered wasting anything." I laugh and splash water at him. "What?" He laughs.

I swim away and Jim swims after me. We splash and swim around each other. The sun is shining with a clear sky above us and the water is so clear I can easily see our feet and the stones and shells below. This really is paradise. I can't help but echo his comment as I think that there's worse ways I could spend my time than splashing around with a gorgeous man in one of the world's most gorgeous destinations.

I need to quell those thoughts, though. This is for a couple of days...nothing more, nothing less. He still lied. He's still a pilot. The fact that he lied and is *using* me this trip adds more weight to my theory about avoiding pilots.

Slowly, the rest of the family comes out to join us. Martha is in the most modest black swimsuit that appears to be more of dress. Bianca is in a one piece with a cute sheer wrap as she plays in the sand with Georgina. Dex swims around a bit, but then joins his wife and child on the beach. Even though I'm here on false pretense, it is nice to be with such a large group on vacation.

"Want to swim out to deeper waters? Maybe let me get you even more wet..."

I bite the inside of my cheek as I turn my attention back to Jim. "Jimmy, dearest, didn't you forget your mommy is watching? I'm a good Greek girl, remember?"

I laugh to myself as I swim away and hear him grumble in Greek.

When the sun begins to set, we head back to the house. There's only one bathroom for all four of us, so I allow Martha to go shower first. Yia-Yia didn't swim today and doesn't need to shower, so I head to the shower when Martha is finished. The water comes out *ice* cold. Instead of him being concerned with my scream of complete shock, I can hear Jimmy laughing outside the door.

"Most of the homes run off solar panels. There's probably no more hot water."

ARROGANT ARRIVAL

I shut off the water and step out of the shower. I can wait until tomorrow when the sun is shining again to take a shower.

The next morning, I go to take my shower. The water pressure isn't strong, but at least it's nice and hot, so I'm not complaining. I lather shampoo into my hair and scrub the salt from the sea out of my scalp. I lose my balance for a moment when I feel the ground shake. What the hell was that? I hurry and try to rinse the shampoo from my face.

Bang! Bang! A fist pounds on the door so I turn off the water so I can hear. "Jolene, come on! Get out! We've got to hurry outside! Earthquake!"

Did Jim just say...earthquake?

The whole house shakes again, causing my shampoo bottle to fall off the shelf. *"Jolene!* Are you okay?"

I hurry out of the shower. "Yes. I'm coming." I grab a towel and wrap it around me as I rush out the door still dripping wet with soap suds on me. "Let me grab—"

"We don't have time, Jo!" Jim grabs my hand and leads me toward the stairs. He lets go of my hand, allowing me to go first down the staircase. We begin hurrying down. I don't even have time to put clothes on, so yeah, this is awkward. The stairs are marble and I'm still soaking wet, so it shouldn't have come as a shock when I slip and skip two steps, busting my ass on the landing.

And I'm naked. In all my naked gloriousness, I'm spread eagle on the stairs during an earthquake with my pretend Greek boyfriend. I couldn't write this story if I tried.

Jim hurries to my side and wraps the towel around me. "Are you okay?"

The whole building shakes again. "Yeah, could've been worse. The ceiling could've fallen on me."

That's when I notice the front door is open. *I wish the ceiling would've fallen on me.* Yia-Yia is making her cross sign again, but for some reason, I don't think it's for everyone's safety from the earthquake. It's apparently for my naked soul. We get outside and of course, Jim's entire family and then some are all there. I wrap the towel tightly around me as I embarrassingly look around. It seems that the entire neighborhood is gawking at me. I turn to Bianca who offers me a sympathetic smile. I return with a close-lipped smile, my face a mask of shame, "I was in the shower."

She nods. "I guessed that."

I can't help but notice that Dex will *not* look my way. I fidget and turn to Bianca again. "I fell coming down the stairs."

"I also saw that. Are you alright?"

"No. I'm really not. But my pride is wounded more than my ass. Far more."

Jim grins. "I don't know why. I mean, you have a great kolo. Hey, and at least you shaved." *Surprisingly, I feel slightly better. At least I was well-groomed when my vagina made her Greece public debut.*

I notice the ground hasn't moved any more. In fact, I don't think it's shaken the entire time we've been outside. Someone yells something in Greek, and everyone goes back to their houses. My jaw drops. "I almost died from humiliation and falling down the stairs, and that's it?"

Martha frowns at me, "Did you want destruction? People to lose their homes...their lives? Be grateful that's all it was." Ouch. She doesn't wait for my response.

Jimmy gives me a sheepish smile. "Earthquakes are common in Greece. Sometimes, for the little ones, we don't even leave the house."

"I didn't want destruction... it's just. I don't even know. I guess if I'd known it wasn't going to be that serious, I wouldn't have literally busted my ass to get out here so fast."

Speaking of...I'm still standing out in the street in only a small white towel. I hurry inside and up the stairs. I'm pleased to report that on the way back up, I only slipped once and hurt my knee. But nobody saw my tush this time, at least.

So I'll take that as a win.

After I get dressed, I go downstairs to find a stunning brunette sitting on the couch. Martha is serving her a cup of coffee and a plate with cookies on it. Martha beams at me, "Jo, this is Voula. She's an old family friend."

She looks younger than me, so not sure how *old* of a friend she is. "Hello, Voula."

"Yia sas Jo. Welcome to Greece."

"Thank you." I go and sit on the chair next to the couch.

"Have you had a chance to explore the country any?"

Before I can answer Voula, Martha chimes in. "Only swimming at the beach behind the condo. Not sure what Jimmy plans on doing with her while they're here."

Voula smiles at me. "I was planning to go out this afternoon with Jimmy. Maybe he can bring you along. I wouldn't mind."

Excuse me? Martha chuckles and playfully pinches Voula cheek. "You always were such a sweet girl."

Jimmy enters the room, and his thick, dark eyebrows rise at the sight of *sweet* Voula. He looks to his mother, back to Voula, to me, and then back to his mother. He's wearing a light blue button-up, the top buttons are open, exposing his collar bone and part of his strong chest, the sleeves rolled up to his forearms, and dark navy slacks. He isn't wearing shoes, and I can't figure out why his bare feet look sexy. I think I was out in the sun too long. He raises his chin and strolls into the room with his hands in his pants pockets.

"Yia sas Voula. Surprised to see you."

Voula smiles and bats her eyelashes. "I hope it's a happy surprise, Jimmy mou."

Jimmy mou! I dip my chin and tilt my head so I can still look up at him and bat my eyelashes, "Jimmy mou, didn't *we* have plans tonight? I'm afraid Boula here is in for a surprise."

Martha gasps. "Voula. V – V – *oula.*"

I grin and feign shock. "That's not how I said it?"

Jimmy saunters toward me and smiles. "Koritsi mou." He kisses me on the forehead and then turns to Voula. "I'm sorry. This is a bad time. Maybe you can come visit us again, or we all can go out for coffee some time. I did promise my koritsi here a night out."

ARROGANT ARRIVAL

Martha rushes toward us and claps her hands. "Maybe Voula can join! She was so sweet to already invite Jo out."

That's not exactly how it played out...

"I'd love to!" Voula smiles widely at Jim.

Jim hesitates, and I can see the panic in his eyes. "Really, Jo and I need a night alone, just the two of us. I'm sure you understand. In fact, we need to get going." Jimmy walks over a grabs a pair of shoes by the door and starts putting them on.

"Jimmy mou, where are you going? Voula just got here." Martha then starts speaking quickly to Jimmy in Greek. Voula smirks at me. I stand up and walk over to Jimmy. I wrap my arms around his waist and kiss his neck.

"I'm ready when you are."

Martha's eyes go wide, while Voula crosses her arms and pouts. Jimmy places his arm around my waist and leads me toward the door. "We'll be back later tonight, Ma."

Jimmy drives us to an area of the island with lots of little restaurants and cafés by the water. He parks the car and we begin walking. He reaches for my hand, but I avoid his by crossing my arms as we walk. I'm still angry with him, and I want to stay that way. If I let my guard down and start believing in this fantasy, I'll only get hurt again.

We walk by an ice cream shop, and Jim nods his head toward it. "Let's get some."

I never turn down ice cream, so I agree. Because—duh—it's ice cream. The place is very modern and open. The room is bright colors with bright lights. A little Greek elderly man smiles at us. I read all the flavors and struggle to decide.

"You can choose more than one flavor." Jim smiles.

"That's true." I decide on vanilla, pistachio, and lemon. Jim gets chocolate and butter pecan caramel.

We take our cups of ice cream and begin walking. Every now and then Jim reaches over and quickly swipes a bite from my ice cream. We come to an old wooden bridge that reminds me of a Venetian style. Jim stops in the center of the bridge and looks out into the blue water.

I lick my spoon and then pop my lips. "You've grown quiet."

"I'm thinking," Jim says while not looking at me.

"Well, that can't be good."

He gives a humorless chuckle. "Are you ever going to loosen your guard with me?"

"Nope." I go back to focusing on my ice cream.

"You know I have a right to be angry as well. You didn't even give me a chance to explain."

With ice cream still in my mouth, I say, "I asked you twice what you did, and you never answered. I said I didn't want a relationship with a pilot, and you remained quiet. Yet this is my fault?"

Jim takes a bite of his ice cream and continues to stare out into the water. People walk by us laughing, I can hear a soccer game on a television off in the distance at one of the cafés, and there's the sound of waves. Jim finally turns to me. "I was scared you'd immediately reject me. I wanted a chance to prove myself, at least."

ARROGANT ARRIVAL

"Prove what? We only had sex."

"It wasn't only sex. It started out that way...but you felt something. We both felt something. Either way, I just wanted a chance."

"Well, you got it, and you blew it."

"Yeah, I did, didn't I?"

We go back to eating our ice cream and looking out over the water. Off in the distance, I see a cruise ship. I can't help but wonder what stories are aboard that ship. Where is it going? Where has it been? How many couples are on board living their best lives?

"We are going to have to up our game."

I'm not too thrilled by Jim's tone. "What does that mean?"

"My mother is going to keep bringing women around. The whole point of you being here is for them to believe I've already found one."

"Jim, she doesn't like me. I think she's going to keep on either way. Sorry, pal, but unless you get married, I doubt she's going to stop. Even then it's iffy."

I immediately regret my words when I see the light bulb come on over Jim's head. "Abso-fucking-lutely not. This isn't Vegas! We aren't getting married, you jerk. Aren't people here more traditional? We might not even be able to get out of it."

"Not married, Jo. Just engaged." When I continue to stare at him, hoping he'll crack a smile and say 'kidding', he only smiles wider. Then slowly, in the middle of the bridge, Jim gets down on one knee. He sits his cup of ice cream down next to him and takes my hand in between his sticky fingers.

"Jolene Tanner... Tannerelos," I hate how my heart just skipped a beat, especially when he used that

93

damn accent on my fake last name. "Will you do me the honor of being my fake fiancée for the next six days? Make me the happiest and luckiest Greek bastard... just for one week. Then you can break my heart and flee this land."

A few people stop on the bridge and take their phones out. I hear the clicking of cameras and a few 'awws'. The rest of what they say is in Greek, so I am sure they misunderstood him about the whole 'fake' part of it all. I force a smile and speak through gritted teeth, "Get. Up."

"Not until you agree..." He turns his head as a cat wanders up and begins loudly licking at his ice cream. I can't help but stare and giggle. Jim shoos the cat and then turns back to me. "Not until you agree to be my fake Greek bride."

Smiling as sweetly as possible, I say, "But, darling, do you even have a ring? Do you honestly think they'll believe it?"

"This is spontaneous, which makes it even more romantic. Or it would be if I didn't have to explain it to you." He kisses my knuckles and it causes my stomach to dip. With his lips barely above my skin, he looks up at me through those dark, long lashes, and in a low voice speaks. "I can't promise you forever right now, but I will promise you the best damn six days."

I turn over the hand he's holding and take his chin between my fingers. I bend down and kiss him on the lips. The crowd cheers. I pull away and whisper, "Yes."

Jim jumps up and lifts me in the air, spinning me around. I laugh and hold on to him. After he gently places me back down, he smiles to the crowd and we both offer a little wave.

ARROGANT ARRIVAL

"I'll go buy you a ring right now."

"You don't have to buy me a ring."

We pick up our ice cream bowls and take them to a trash can at the end of the bridge. Jim then takes my hand and practically drags me through people walking the streets.

"Where are we going?" I call out.

"You're right. They won't believe it without a ring." He stops in front of a souvenir shop. "This will work."

"Are you kidding me?"

"It's after two. None of the jewelry shops are open in the middle of the day. These places stay open for tourists. Besides, you said I didn't even have to get you a ring. Now you want to be picky?"

"You're right. Why be picky now when I'm with you?" I brush past him and into the little shop. They have some very pretty jewelry that is supposedly crafted here in Greece and made from genuine stone.

"See one you like? I'll purchase whatever your heart desires."

I'm positive he has not seen some of these price tags. I smile and ask to see this ring that is two-toned metal, a silver band with a golden vine of leaves intertwining around the band. In the center is a sapphire.

The ring just so happens to fit perfectly. I show Jim and he smiles. "It seems like this is fate again." He asks if this is the one, and I nod. He looks to the lady behind the counter and smiles. "We'll take this one."

"Very nice. That will be a thousand euros."

Jim's smug smile falters, but mine remains in place as he looks over at me. I saw the price tag and knew exactly how much. Jim extends his hand out and begins speaking in Greek to the lady. Her eyes widen and she giggles. They exchange a few words with amused identical expressions, and then he hands her some cash. *Wait a minute...*

She walks around the register and takes my face in hers. She kisses each side of my face and keeps speaking excitedly in Greek. Jim hugs her and then begins guiding me out the door.

"What the hell was that?" I ask as soon as we're away from the store.

"I got us a discount."

"Yeah, but how and why?"

"What do you mean how and why? No offense, but I wasn't about to pay that for a ring that we don't even know if it'll turn your finger green. But I got us the 'I'm Greek' discount and 'this is an engagement ring' discount."

We step back on the bridge and as we're crossing I ask mimicking his accent, "What's the *I'm Greek* discount?"

"Greek tourist places don't charge their own people as much."

When we're back at the center of the bridge, Jim places a hand out and stops me from walking. He guides me to the side of the bridge and stands so close to me, his legs are on either side of mine. Taking the bag from my hand, he reaches in and removes the little ring box. He removes the ring and then tosses the box back in the bag. He takes my ring finger, and without breaking eye contact with me, he slowly slides the ring on.

"Can I at least kiss you?"

"Seems it would be the appropriate thing to do right now."

ARROGANT ARRIVAL

"It does. It feels like the thing to do."

"Then do it." I raise my lips toward his.

Jim first kisses my finger adorned with the ring, and then his lips crash to mine. His tongue pushes against my lips and I part them, granting him further access. As his tongue slides against mine, I feel my knees becoming weak. He presses himself harder against me, and I feel his excitement.

"God, Jolene." He leans his forehead against mine. "You taste so sweet."

"It's from the ice cream." I breathe out.

We both chuckle as we hold onto each other. "Come on," Jim laughs as he tugs my hand.

When we arrive to the house, there's a group of people sitting in the living room. Martha smiles at us and proudly says, "I have some stuffed tomatoes fresh out of the oven in the kitchen."

It's almost nine at night. Everybody loves to eat late here. Instead of voicing that thought, I say "Thank you. Sounds delicious."

I notice that Voula is still here, but instead of scowling at me, she's giving a sour look to another stunning young woman. Said woman stands up and walks toward Jim with open arms. "Jimmy," she coos with her seductive Greek accent. "I was hoping I wouldn't have to wait all night for you." *Gag me.*

"Eleni." He smiles and lightly kisses her on each cheek. "So nice to see you."

"You are certainly a nice sight to see. You've grown, in all the right places, over the years." She squeezes his biceps. "It's been too long," she pouts.

I pull his arm to me and wedge myself between them. "A lot can change in that much time. I'm Jolene... his fiancée."

A round of audible gasps are heard, along with what sounds like glass breaking in the kitchen.

CHAPTER 11
Jolene

Dear Journal,

I'm engaged. Normally, I'd call my mother because this would make her year. Her only daughter won't be an old maid forever. Unfortunately, since this is simply another lie to add to the web Jim and I are weaving, I'll leave her out of this. We're limiting our lying to only his side of the family. To celebrate our engagement, Jimmy decided to take me to Athens for the day and an overnight trip. The city is definitely crowded, and there's so much to see and do. I was actually missing the charm of the spacious island and blue waters. Jim smiled at me and said he knew just the place to take me. If you ever visit Greece, I'd highly recommend where he took me: Sounio. It's a little ways out of the city, and actually in a town called Attica, there at the southernmost tip of the peninsula in

Cape Sounio is the Temple of Poseidon. The remaining white marble columns stand tall and elegant against the contrast of the blue ocean it's perched above. The site takes my breath away. It's peaceful to stand there high above the rest of the world and look out into the vast blue sea. Although Athena got the more elaborate temple with the Parthenon in the middle of the city of Athens, I find that Poseidon got the best view, by far. The sea surrounds the temple on three sides. Every time a light breeze would come, I could almost feel an energy there.

"Like this better?" Jim asked me.

"I'm honestly speechless. This is...incredible."

"Huh. That's funny."

"Why?"

"Because I was just thinking the exact same thing, only it was about you."

Whether he meant the words or not, my heart fluttered. I couldn't be sure if it was the high altitude of where we are standing, or the smile he gave me, but I did begin to feel a little lightheaded.

"Dress a little fancy," Jim calls out.

I wrap the towel around me, even though it's nothing he hasn't seen, touched, and ... well, it's nothing new to him, and open the bathroom door. "For

ARROGANT ARRIVAL

what? Besides, I only brought one dress with me, so it'll have to do."

"I'm taking you somewhere nice tonight. We're celebrating, after all."

"Fake celebrating our fake engagement?"

Jim strolls up to me with one hand in his dress slacks pockets. The other hand reaches out and rips the towel from my body. He pulls me close to him. I try to wiggle free, "Let go. I'm getting you wet."

"Hah, ain't that the truth. Besides, that happened the moment you opened the door in nothing but a towel."

"Ugh. You're so immature and gross."

"Possibly. Yet, here we are. You're engaged to me, even. What were you thinking?"

"I ask myself that constantly. And, it's fake. It's based on a lie, just like this entire trip."

"Tonight isn't. Tonight, I'm taking you out to celebrate that I get to spend some of the best days of my life with the most incredible and gorgeous woman. That's not a lie, Jo. Despite how we got here, let's just be happy that we are here. Together."

Well, how the hell do I respond to that? I lick my lips and his nostrils flare. He releases his hold on me and steps back. "Get dressed or we won't make it."

Jim takes me to a rooftop restaurant. We're seated at the edge of the balcony with a clear view of the city of Athens and the Parthenon. We arrive just as the sun is getting ready to set. I smile as I take it all in, the ancient civilization and modern world all blended in the beauty and culture of Greece.

"Do you like it?"

I laugh at his ridiculous question. "How could I not?"

"Why is that so funny? Obviously, this is quite amazing, but so am I. And it's obvious you don't like me."

No, Jim, far worse. I think I'm falling in love with you.

CHAPTER 12

Jimmy

I'm literally smacked awake by a pillow. I open my eyes to find Yia-Yia standing over me with a frown. "It's time for church. Don't argue. We *need* a divine intervention in this family." She shuffles out of the room and I can't help but smile. Ma and Yia-Yia wasted no time in tearing into me when we got back from Athens last night. They're convinced that being in a plane all the time with the high altitude has finally destroyed my brain.

I knock on Jolene's bedroom door. She answers wearing only a towel—another damn towel—and I almost crumble to my knees. Yia-Yia walks by and shakes her head, mumbling in Greek and doing the cross-signing thing again. *"Doesn't she ever wear clothes? I see her naked butt more than I see my own."*

I have no response to that because the visual of my grandma's naked butt is a total and complete cockblock.

"Um, we leave for church in about an hour." I try to focus on her eyes before I pitch a tent in my pants.

"Tell her to make sure she wears a dress or skirt!" My yia-yia yells out in Greek as she goes down the stairs. *"And it better not be short. We don't want her embarrassing the family any more than she already has."*

I smile at Jolene. "Women are expected to wear a dress or skirt. Modest length."

Jolene raises her eyebrows. "Modest length."

I nod. "Do you want me to sit in here while you try some on? I like to be helpful and available for comment and critique."

Jolene shakes her head and slams the door in my face. *Guess that was a no.* I go downstairs to the kitchen where Yia-Yia and Ma are preparing food for lunch. They always prepare too much food, but there's way more company than usual. Ma notices me staring and smiles. "The priest is coming over for lunch. I told him you were engaged, and he wants to bless the union."

Yia-Yia mumbles something inaudible, so I don't comment. The Greek churches have a lot of priests and sometimes we go to different ones. I'm curious to see which one Ma has been talking to.

"Which one?"

"Father Giorgos."

"Oh, Ma...Father George? Really? Couldn't you have invited Father Earl or Stanley?"

Ma walks up and pops me in the back of the head. "Don't speak poorly of the priest. He is a man of God. Father Giorgos is a little old—"

ARROGANT ARRIVAL

"The man is senile and old as Moses." I leap out of the way before she can come at me again. Yia-Yia laughs, clearly agreeing with me. She's practically blind, but even she can see the man has a screw loose.

Yia-Yia starts mumbling something about a tight skirt, and I turn around to find Jolene. She's wearing a long, fitted navy skirt with a white, long-sleeve button up. Her long, ebony hair is straight and smooth flowing down her back.

"I'll have to wear the skirt from my uniform. I didn't pack any long dresses or skirts," she tells the room. "Will this be alright?"

"You look very pretty, koritsi." Ma beams. Yia-Yia shrugs and goes back to peeling potatoes.

"Beautiful. Come on, let's go ahead and get going."

Ma, Yia-Yia, Jolene, and I walk outside. I jog over to knock on Bianca's condo door. They come out and we start walking toward the church. Jolene leans closer to me, "Shouldn't we take the car so Yia-Yia doesn't have to walk to the church."

I whisper back, "Don't let her hear you say that. If we're walking, she's walking. Besides, she'll argue that there's no need to waste gas for such a short distance. She may have a walker, but she could probably outlast all of us. It's only a block."

When we arrive at the church, I tell Jolene that women and men sit on different sides. Her eyes widen, but Bianca takes her hand. "You can sit next to me. I don't speak Greek, either, but don't worry. We'll just stand and sit whenever everyone else does."

"I really like Bianca," Jolene whispers to me.

Jolene

When the service has ended, everyone scatters. I scan for Jimmy, but turn to find I've now lost Bianca. A beautiful woman approaches me and makes a point of looking me up and down. She speaks a few words in Greek. I smile and shake my head, "I'm sorry. I don't speak Greek."

She laughs, but it's not sweet at all. It's definitely a bitch laugh, and she continues to speak in Greek. Two other women join her and now they are all laughing. They nod in agreement to whatever it is she's saying.

I don't have to take this shit. I turn to walk around her, but she side steps in front of me. I'm about to slap the bitch out of my way when Jimmy runs up. "Jolene."

The Greek bitch in front of me plasters the most ridiculous smile on her face. "Yia, Dimitrios."

"Yia sou, Pamela."

She begins speaking to *Dimitrios* in a completely different tone than the one she used for me. Oh, so the bitch just leveled up. Now I'm pissed. I cross my arms and narrow my eyes. So she thinks she can use Greek to exclude me. Well, let's see how she likes it when I use English to exclude *her*.

"Jimmy, I'm not too crazy about this *woman* and would like to leave."

"I'm not too crazy about you either, American," Pamela now speaks in perfect English. Like proper English. She raises her chin and smirks.

ARROGANT ARRIVAL

"If you know English, then why did you speak to me only in Greek? Too much of a coward to say it to my face so I'd understand you?"

"No. I'll tell you." She takes a step closer, invading my space. "I was just saying how it's ridiculous that you don't even know the language of your people. That is, if you really are Greek. And how is someone like Dimitrios slumming it with the likes of you? He could do so much better."

Jimmy shakes his head, "Stop. Let's go." He takes my hand, but I jerk free.

"You think you're good enough?" I look her up and down exactly how she did to me.

She smiles wider. "His family seems to think so. I already have the approval of his mother—something you obviously do not have."

Jimmy steps between us, "But I don't. Pamela, just because Thea Maria and Ma are trying to play Cupid doesn't mean anything. I *chose* Jolene. I brought her here to be with me. Not to be set up with anyone else here."

I peek my head from around him and smirk. "Looks like the only approval I need is his. And I've got it. Face it, *Pamela*...I doubt he'll be inviting your kolo to America."

Jimmy looks up to the ceiling and makes a cross. "Jolene, we're still in church."

I look up to see Jesus's face looking down on me. I make the cross like I've seen everyone else doing and say a silent prayer for forgiveness. When in Rome, right? Or, should I say, when in Greece. Jimmy tugs my hand and mumbles, "Let's go, Jo, before we get kicked out of the church or lightning strikes us down."

I turn and give Pamela a wave, making sure my engagement ring is in clear view before we exit the building.

As we're walking to the house with the others, Jimmy has us hang at the back of the group. "I'm sorry about Pamela."

"That was what you were worried about, wasn't it? Why you asked me to accompany you here? I mean, we were kind of expecting it."

"Yeah, but I didn't like seeing her talk to you that way."

"It's okay."

"Well, we're about to be in for another treat. Father Giorgos, or George in English, is a little different. He's kind of crazy, but he's a likable guy. Just be prepared."

"For what?"

Jimmy sighs. "Anything and everything. He is going to bless our union."

We step into the condo and go to the kitchen. I make myself busy helping set the table and pouring glasses of wine and water. A knock at the door has Martha running to the door. I hear her voice loud and clear as she welcomes the priest into the house. Everyone bows and kisses his hand, so I do, too, when he comes over to me.

I have no idea what he's saying to me, but his eyes are kind and his smile is sincere so I just smile and nod. Jimmy comes over, beaming, and then tells me to have a seat. We all sit as Martha places the food on the table. Father George blesses the meal and then we begin placing food on our plate. For the most part, all the conversation is in Greek. Which is fine with me,

ARROGANT ARRIVAL

I can focus on eating and less on conversation that I know nothing about.

"You are a very lovely woman, Jo-lene."

I look up, shocked that the priest just spoke in English to me. He gives a little high-pitched laugh and then coughs. "'Scuse me. You see, I studied in America many, many years ago. My English not so good now, but..." He holds up a single finger and taps his temple. "I still remember some."

"Where in America did you study?"

"Boston."

"Wow. Did you like it in the States?"

"Oh yes, yes. I had always hoped to return but ah, what are you going to do? Time waits for no one. You remember this. God wants us to live life and give life. I think you and Dimitrios will make wonderful babies."

Excuse me, what? Babies were definitely not part of this scenario.

Jimmy releases a nervous laugh. "Papas, forgive me, but how does you going back to America relate to us becoming parents. We're not even married." Jim leans closer to me and takes my hand that's resting on the table. He kisses my knuckles and whispers. "Yet."

Lying in front of a priest seems to be a whole new level of wrong. I ease my hand from his grasp and refuse to meet his eyes. I look at the priest and try to smile.

"More importantly, we're not–" I stop short. "Not ready to get married... right away."

Father George does his little high-pitch chuckle again. He points a finger at Jimmy. "You'll marry her soon. You smart boy, Dimitri." He reaches over and pats Jim's cheek. "You'll marry this woman. And then you'll plant your seed many times over. I know this."

Dex starts coughing and Bianca downs her wine in an attempt to not burst out laughing. Those traitors. Yia-Yia is making a cross, and I can only assume praying...hopefully for me and not praying that I drop her grandson like a hot rock. Martha is staring wide-eyed, looking back and forth between me and Jim. I pray that this conversation is over...but alas, my prayers go unanswered, probably because I didn't do the cross-thingy on my chest, because the conversation is far from over.

Father George stares intently at me across the table. "Dimitri is a good man. He is a good farmer. Let him tend to your garden and bury his seed deep for many years to come." He cuts up a piece of meat on his plate and then points his fork laden with a big chunk of meat at me. "Have you been baptized?"

"Um, yeah. When I was younger in the First Baptist Church."

"That's okay, my child. We baptize you here, so you marry Dimitrios in Greek church. Now, let us pray."

Dear God, I pray for strength to get through the rest of this week.

CHAPTER 13

Jolene

"We only have a few days left." Jimmy stands in my doorway. I'm reading on my bed with the balcony door open, a light breeze blowing the curtain. "Time really flies when you're having fun, huh?"

"Oh yeah." I turn the page. "I've gone from a fake relationship, to a fake engagement, and now apparently a baptism is in my foreseeable future, along with a Greek wedding and you tending to my *garden*."

Jim laughs. "Come on. We don't have time for all that."

I tilt my head. "Are you sure about that? You seem to work pretty quick."

"I mean – there's always time for *plowing,* but not sure I can even get a Greek baptism and wedding in. Those are pretty big events."

"What have I gotten myself into?" I mumble.

"I promised you before that I'd take you to a romantic destination. So, how about tomorrow morning we hop on a ferry boat or take a puddle jumper over to one of the islands?"

I set my book down and turn on my side. "You don't have to do that, Jim. I'm having a nice time."

"You don't have to lie. I'll go book us some tickets for tomorrow. We can stay away for a few days, I mean, you've endured so much already. Or are you afraid to be alone with me? Scared you won't be able to resist my charms?" He wiggles his eyebrows and walks out before I can come up with a quick retort. Resist his charms, ugh. At least those are days I won't have to worry about running into little sirens and a priest who might try to baptize me.

I hear a noise outside my balcony and head over to see what it is. Martha is hanging the laundry so I walk outside to join her and pick up a towel. "Can I help?"

"Sure." She keeps working. We're silent for a long while. I know Yia-Yia isn't fond of me, but I get the impression that Martha isn't crazy about me either. She's just less vocal about her disdain. Wearing my sassy pants this morning, I decide what can it hurt, I'm never going to see this woman again probably, so I have to ask.

"Martha? Have I offended you?"

"Yes." She keeps working. I wasn't expecting blunt from Martha.

"Are you going to tell me how?" I pick up another towel and pin it to the line.

"No." She shakes another towel and pins it.

"I can't make things better if—"

She throws a towel down and turns her dark eyes on me. "You want to know why? Fine. I tell you." She

ARROGANT ARRIVAL

shakes her finger at me. "You no love my son. You're with him and because of that, he can't find real love. If you love him, fine. But I'm not okay watching him look at you the way he does, but you no look back. I love my son. He's my only boy. I want to see him happy and in love. Look me in the eye right now and tell me under God's eye that you love him?"

"What makes you think I don't love him?"

"The way you acted over what the priest said. The way you don't return his touches. I see everything. I only want what's best for him." She stomps away from me at that final word.

Bianca walks out onto the balcony from their connecting condo with Georgina in her arms. They look out over the ocean and I feel like I'm intruding on a sweet moment between them. As I turn to go back inside, I hear, "Jo! Hey, we were just about to go down to the beach. Would you like to join us?"

"I don't want to interrupt your family time..."

"Nonsense. Besides, you're engaged to Jimmy, so you're practically family. He's never even had serious girlfriends, so you must be pretty special."

Special cover up. "Well, alright then. I'll meet you all downstairs."

I throw on my swimsuit, a cover up, and grab a towel. Ma and Yia-Yia immediately stop speaking when I pass them in the kitchen. *You were speaking in Greek, it's not like I understood anyway so it was pointless to stop talking,* I want to say, but I offer a single wave as I hear them mumble kolo again. Jesus, I'll never live that down. A swim will do me good, both mentally and physically, though...and hopefully help me relax.

When I walk out the door, Dex, Bianca, and Georgina are waiting for me. Dex has his shirt unbuttoned and his amazing abs on display. No wonder Georgina is absolutely the most gorgeous baby ever. Just look at her parents.

We walk down to the beach, and I throw a towel on a chair. I'm taken by surprise when little Georgina reaches for me.

"Do you want to hold her?" Bianca asks.

"Sure. If that's alright?"

"More than alright. I'll be able to actually apply my sunscreen." Bianca hands me Georgina, but Dex grabs the sunscreen instead.

"I'll be happy to oblige. You've had your hands full. You relax while I get me a hand full." She laughs and blushes. He's definitely a charmer, just like Jimmy is.

Jimmy? When did I start using his nickname? Must be something in the air.

Dex immediately begins rubbing sunscreen on her, and it's slightly awkward for me. Especially when Bianca releases a little moan. *Okay. Time for me and little Georgina to find something to distract ourselves with...preferably down near the water.* I walk a little ways and sit down on the warm sand with Georgina on my lap. I begin making a pile as the waves come in, just enough to wet the sand nice and good, and her chubby little hands smash it. She giggles and claps, so I do it again.

"She loves it, Jo. I think she's really taken a liking to you." I don't look back, but I can hear the smile in Bianca's voice.

"I've taken a liking to her, too! She's absolutely adorable." I give Georgina a little hug before I go back to making another pile for her to smash. This is the relaxation that I needed. The simplicity of making a baby giggle is medicine for my soul that I didn't know I needed.

"Want to join me for a swim?" I hear Dex ask Bianca. She hesitates, so I turn around to look at her.

"You two go have some time for yourselves. We're fine." I look down at the happy little baby on my lap, "Aren't we? Yeah? We're having fun, aren't we?"

Bianca laughs as she stands up. She and Dex take off into the water, giggling and splashing each other like teenagers. A few minutes later, a shadow looms over me and Georgina. I look up to find Jim watching us.

"Bianca left you alone with Georgina?"

"Yes...why?"

Jim sits down next to me and tickles Georgina under her chin. "She never leaves her alone with anyone. Must say something about you?"

I roll my eyes. "We're not really alone, Jim. They're right there." I point to them as Bianca climbs on to Dex's back laughing. I smile, but it doesn't reach my eyes. "That's what love looks like."

"Yeah, they're pretty crazy about each other."

I look to Jim, "Have you ever been in love?"

He keeps his eyes on the ocean when he answers. "In the Greek language, there's different words for different types of love. I've experienced some forms of love, but the kind you're describing...no."

I notice a difference in his eyes. They're not playful and full of mischief anymore. No, now they're sad. I reach over and take his hand and give him a squeeze.

"My friend's tell me that my Mr. Right will arrive someday, so I'm sure your Mrs. Right will too."

Jim gives a humorless laugh. "Unfortunately for you, you've got to deal with this arrogant Greek bastard until then."

I quickly cover Georgina's little ears. "Sshh, a child is present."

He laughs, "She's not even talking yet."

"Geek Bas-ard"

Oh no, no, no! This is bad! "Jimmy...did she just say..."

"Hey...you called me Jimmy." He grins widely.

I roll my eyes. "I'm more worried about what name *she* called you!"

"Geek Bas-ard!"

Jim shushes her. "No, koukla mou, Greek *must*ard." He nods. "Not bas—"

"*Jimmy!*" I hiss.

"*Must*ard," he continues.

She giggles. "Greek..." Jimmy nods encouragingly. "Greek bastard!"

Of course, right then, Bianca and Dex would walk up. They could've swam for another ten minutes but nooooo. Dex grins proudly, "Is Georgina speaking her first word?"

Bianca beams and kneels down. "What is it baby? Did you say Ma-Ma?"

"Greek bastard!" I cringe when I hear the sweet little voice speak. To my surprise, Bianca jumps up and swats Dex's arm.

"I told you to watch your language! I knew she was listening when you yelled at that driver."

ARROGANT ARRIVAL

"He cut me off!"

Jimmy and I look at each other and give a single nod. We'll be taking that little secret to the grave for sure. I hand Georgina back to Bianca. Jimmy and I stand together. "I wasn't for sure if that's what she was saying."

"Yeah, it just came out of nowhere." He shakes his head as he feigns disappointment. "What are you teaching your child, you two?"

Bianca fusses over baby Georgina, encouraging her to say Ma-Ma, but it's useless.

"Greek bastard."

"We're gonna go now," Jimmy says as he throws an arm over my shoulders. I nod in agreement.

As we walk away, we both burst into a fit of giggles. Instead of removing his arm, Jim wraps the other one around me. Without words, he brings his lips to mine and I welcome them. When he pulls away, I smile...an authentic, genuine smile.

"I'm really glad to know it wasn't my fault her first word was Greek bastard," he whispers.

"I doubt you helped matters any by repeating it twice. Mustard...is that even a thing in Greece?" I start laughing again.

He shrugs like *what's a guy to do* and brings his lips back to mine.

"I'm really glad to hear you call me Jimmy." He gives me a sweet kiss on the lips. When he pulls away, he leads me toward the condo. I look up to find Yia-Yia watching us. I give a little wave, but she continues to just watch me. They said her eyesight is really bad, that she certainly couldn't see anything at a distance, but something tells me she does...and that, like Martha, she sees everything.

Martha walks in the living room all excited. "We are going to have family over tonight. Maria is coming and she's bringing a few other friends we haven't seen in years. Along with her goddaughter, Pamela"

Pamela. I really don't want to deal with her again. The nerve. We just announced we were engaged. I'm going to have to up my game to help Jimmy, or they'll try to have those two married by the end of this trip. There's a buzz from the doorbell and Martha claps. "That's them!"

I hear a round of "Yia sas" and "Yia." At least eight Greek people walk in the room. Counting us, with Bianca, Georgina, and Dex, the room is full. Martha offers drinks while everyone chats. Everyone is very friendly and sweet. Jimmy translates for most, but a few know English. After a while, Dex offers to order gyros and souvlaki for everyone. There's a buzz again at the door a little later, and I'm excited, expecting food. Instead, my stomach turns sour when in walks Pamela with the same two women from church. Her olive skin practically glows from kisses from the sun. Her wavy, chestnut-colored hair hangs down past her shoulders, her eyebrows are a perfect thick curve, the smoky eye shadow and long black eyelashes accents her honey-colored eyes, and her lips are fire engine red. But...I am not intimated by this ridiculously gorgeous woman. Nope. So what if everyone in this room would rather

ARROGANT ARRIVAL

Jimmy be with her instead of me? So what if she's a Greek goddess come to life who's so gorgeous I almost want to date her? I don't care. Jimmy chose *me*.

She doesn't even hesitate when she goes to sit on the other side of Jimmy. Despite knowing English, she speaks only in Greek to him. It's her way of deliberately excluding me from the conversation. *Would it be wrong to teach Georgina to say Greek bitch and have her go tell Pamela her new word?*

The food arrives and Martha sets up a little buffet for everyone to fix a plate and then sit wherever they can find a spot. Everyone laughs and speaks animatedly. Despite Pamela's presence, the entire evening so far has been really nice.

Wait. I'm not going to let her ruin my vacation, especially when I'm here on false pretenses.

I stand to go throw away my paper plate. When I enter the kitchen, Bianca is there. She beams at me with flushed cheeks and holds up a bottle of wine. "Would you like a glass?"

"Yes, please!"

She laughs at my enthusiasm and begins to pour a glass. She hands it to me, and I take a sip. "This is delicious. You know, I always thought the best wine I've ever had was from Italy but this," I examine my glass, "is pretty darn good."

"Thanks. It's from Theo Vasili's vineyard."

"Oh, have I met him?"

"Maybe. Not sure if I've met him." We both giggle. "I don't know who anyone is. He could be out there for all I know. Jimmy could tell you."

"He does seem to know everyone." *Especially all the women.* "Is Greece everything you were hoping for?"

"And more. We're hoping to do more of the touristy stuff the next couple of days. Then back to work."

"Yeah, you work at a magazine. That must be fun. I majored in journalism in college." Bianca's eyes widen in surprise, so I continue. "True story. I worked at a newspaper but hated it. I got restless. I was still so young and wanted to see the world. I still write some, just in my journal. I love to write about all my trips." I sigh and take another sip of wine. "I love to travel. You know that's the best part about my job, but I hate that it's always go-go-go. That doesn't make sense. I love to go, but I wish I had a little more freedom and not such a chaotic schedule. Like now, I'm so grateful that I'm able to just enjoy Greece instead of just a quick layover."

"You should start a travel blog or work for a magazine. Some places will pay for your travel experiences in exchange for promotion and reviews."

"I wouldn't even know the first thing about starting something like that."

Bianca tilts her head to study me a moment. "I could see about getting you a job at the magazine I work for."

"Wh-what?"

"Yeah. You could even write some articles for our website."

"That would be amazing but, Bianca," I take a deep breath. "What if Jim and I break up? You're doing this now while I'm his girlfriend and you're drinking

ARROGANT ARRIVAL

wine...I mean, let's say we're no longer a couple." *And you're sober.* "Then what?"

Bianca slides down the counter closer to me and whispers. "You mean break up like next week? As soon as you board the plane, this little fake relationship is over?"

"You know?"

Bianca gives me an are-you-kidding-me look, "Jolene, you were our flight attendant and he never once said you were his girlfriend until baggage claim. You two barely spoke on the plane, and when you did, there were death glares coming from you. There's definitely sexual tension, but Jimmy freaked out when I mentioned Thea Martha trying to set him up. Then, all of a sudden—oh look! His girlfriend arrives. But wait—now you're engaged." She snickers and pats my shoulder as she steps away. "The job offer is there regardless of whether or not you and Jimmy are together."

Bianca takes the wine and a few glasses to the living room. Jimmy enters the kitchen and his face lights up when his eyes land on me. "Hey, I wondered where you wandered off to."

When we go back to the living room, everyone is laughing and drinking wine. Jimmy groans and I nudge him. "What's up?"

"One of my cousins knows a couple of tsigganos. He called them to come over and play music."

"Like gypsies? Like fortune tellers and—"

"Not exactly – calling them that is an insult. Gypsy is more of a racist term."

"I'm sorry. I didn't know. So, ts-tsigganos?"

Jim nods and smiles when there's a buzz and in walks four men wearing beige pants, and nice black button ups. They're skin is very tan from the sun, full, wavy short black hair, and dark eyes. Three take a seat together while the one holding a lyra stands. The music begins, and at first I'm not sure what to think. It's a far cry from the hypnotic, upbeat pop music. It's more a mix of ancient tunes and similar to Middle Eastern sounding music. A few of the ladies stand and form a broken circle. With their arms thrown over each other's shoulders, they begin dancing. I clap along with everyone else in the room. A few more people arrive, and everyone is shoulder to shoulder. The melody changes, and then everyone kneels in a circle. One of the guys stands in the center and begins dancing. He slaps his hand on the floor and then jumps in the air. He snaps his fingers and moves to the beat of the music. This isn't typically any music I would listen to just to enjoy the melody, but I can't help but enjoy the dancing and feeling the rhythm. Another gentleman walks in carrying a small looking guitar, maybe some type of a mandolin?

"Jim, who is that and what is that?"

"That's my uncle Vasili. He plays the bouzouki"

Oh, where is Bianca? I found her uncle who has the vineyard. He stands next to the other men and everyone in the room cheers as he begins to play and sing. A woman from the crowd stands up and goes over to join him in the song. The song changes again, and as if on cue, everyone turns toward Jimmy. I don't understand what they're saying, but clearly they want him to stand. He waves his hand and shakes his head, politely declining. I nudge him and smile, "Go on."

"You really want me to?"

"Yeah. Or are you too much of a chicken?"

"Oh, really? I'll show you who's a chicken."

Jimmy stands and takes his place in the center of the circle. The music begins, but there's no vocals, just a catchy beat. Jimmy sways and moves his body all over the circle. He motions for me to scoot forward. I shake my head but notice Pamela easing her way forward. Oh, hell no. So when Jimmy motions for me to move forward again, I slide right up. He whispers for me to dip my head down. I continue to clap with the rest of the group, and then see his foot coming toward me. Quickly, I dip my head and laugh as he swings his leg over me and then twirls around. He drops to his knees, and then leans so far back that he is able to kiss me before he shoots forward. His palm slaps the floor as he yells, "OPA!" He stands and moves again in tune with the music, swaying his arms as his fingers snap. Martha brings a shot glass filled with a clear liquid that holds a strong liquorish smell and places it in the circle. Jimmy dances around the glass before dropping to his knees in front of it. With his hands behind his back, he leans forward and grabs the rim of the glass with his mouth. Turning the glass upwards and drinking the contents and using his hand, he takes the glass and with one knee down, he shouts, "OPA," and throws the glass to the ground, shattering it. Everyone cheers as he stands and goes back to dancing as his shoes crunch on the glass. The song comes to an end and everyone erupts in cheers. Before Jimmy walks out of the circle, he does a quick chicken dance and winks at me as I burst out laughing. Martha comes out with a broom and quickly sweeps up the glass before the music begins again.

"Show off." I tease him.

"You asked for it. *Begged* me to, in fact."

"So you say, sir, so you say." I have a few more glasses of wine and end up joining the half-circle dances. Even though I have no clue what I'm doing, I don't have to worry about what to do with my hands because they're holding on to the shoulders of the people around me. As for my feet, I doubt most people are paying that close of attention to them, anyway. I just bounce and try to follow along the best I can. Jimmy catches my eyes and laughs at me, so I do the only thing I can think of doing...I stick my tongue out. Just then, the song changes and everyone kneels. Except me. I didn't get that memo. So there I am, standing there, towering over everyone with my tongue stuck out. Awkward, to say the least. Before I can join the others by kneeling, a lady who's been in the circle with me urges me to stay and dance. I shake my head no, but she takes my hands and begins to show me some moves that look a lot like belly dancing. Then, she says, "Feel. *Feel*. Music. Feel." When I continue to stare, she sighs and says. "No look. Hear and feel music."

I nod and try to continue to do what she's doing. She shakes her head and places her hands over my eyes. "No look. Keep closed. No see music. Feel."

She removes her hand and I open. When she starts to bring her hand back over my eyes with a 'tsk', I hurry and close them. I feel my face become hot then, and not from the wine. I can *feel* that all eyes are on me right

ARROGANT ARRIVAL

now and I'm slightly embarrassed. But then... I allow myself to listen to the beat. I begin to move and sway, doing what I'd seen her do, but putting my own spin on it. I finally begin to just let myself feel the music. I hear cheers and Greek words of what I assume are encouragement because they sound familiar to what I heard earlier with the other dancers. That's better than the scowls and whispered words I've heard said about me up until this point, I guess.

The woman next to me claps and says, "Bravo koritsi!" I open my eyes as I continue to dance. The woman smiles and nods as she claps. I look over at Jimmy who is biting his bottom lip, his eyes have become heated while watching me. I dance toward him and add an extra pop to my hips. My dance takes on a more seductive tone as I stare only into his blue eyes. The others are just white noise in the background.

The green in his blue eyes glow as they follow the motions of my hips. I lift my hands to the ceiling and slowly make circular motions with my hands. I ease closer toward Jim. My fingertips from my right hand begins to leisurely trail down my extended left arm. When I reach the crook of my elbow, I move my hand to my jaw and slide it down to my neck. The flare from Jim's nostrils and sight of his hands tightening into fists gives me a rush of satisfaction. I'm affecting him this much and we haven't even touched.

Our trance is broken when everyone yells and claps. I turn to see Pamela dancing next to me. She smiles at Jimmy, but he never looks her way. His eyes remain on me, so I go back to dancing. It doesn't matter what she or anyone else does at this point, I'm only dancing for one man. And he is watching only me.

The song transitions into another upbeat melody, sending more dancers to the floor. A hand with sharp nails digs into my arm and pulls me away. Shit, it's Pamela. She drags me out to the balcony. She slides the glass door shut and turns to face me. "You're nothing but an American whore."

"And you're a universal whore." I charge toward her. "What was that? You were trying to dance for *my* fiancé."

Her chin rises in defiance. I narrow my eyes, and the superiority rolling off of her. "What's the matter? Feel threatened?"

I scoff. "I feel embarrassed...for *you*. His eyes never left my body. No matter how hard you tried to throw yourself at him in front of all those people, he never even noticed you. If it's any comfort, at least you have that. He didn't see what a spectacle you made of yourself."

"The joke is you being here as his fiancée. You being here at all must be some kind of charity from Dimitrios. That, or he is trying to play some silly game."

"*Jimmy mou* begged me to come with him. He has begged for my attention while doing everything possible to avoid even speaking to you."

"We'll see." Pamela places her hands on her narrow hips. "I'm bored now."

She turns her back and opens the balcony door. I stand there and watch as she steps inside and closes the balcony door, effectively ending the conversation.

Ridiculous. I can't believe the balls on her. No wonder Jimmy was so desperate to have me be his fake fiancée. They just won't quit.

CHAPTER 14

Jimmy

After that damn sexy dance, the rest of the night went on with everyone grabbing Jolene to dance with them. And I had a freakin' boner for half the night. Unfortunately, I couldn't do anything about it because it was three in the morning by the time everyone left. I helped Ma clean up, and then found Jolene passed out in her bed still wearing her clothes. I cover her up and then go to my room. Still too worked up to go to sleep no matter the time, I sit in my chair and pull my dick out. I close my eyes and see her. I see her black silky hair hanging past her shoulders as her body sways as fluid as a snake slithers. I see her delicate arms extended out as her gorgeous chest bounces slightly as she dances around me. Her deep, honey-colored eyes burn with desire as she stares at me—only me. I'm the luckiest man in the room because I know she's dancing just for me. I grip myself tighter as she dances closer. I pump faster as she comes closer, and closer. She kneels before me and takes me. She takes me in her hand, and it's her hand working me now. Her sweet lips touch my tip, and that's it. I'm finished. What the ever-loving fuck? I open my eyes and look down at where I've come all over my hand. This doesn't bode well that I just experienced premature ejaculation simply in my fantasy of Jolene. I clean off my shame and then fall on to the bed. My last thought is I've got it so damn bad for this girl.

Now what am I going to do about it?

We're on our way to the island of Kefalonia—*alone*. I loaded the car onto the ferry boat, and then go to the upper deck to find Jolene. I don't see her sitting anywhere, so I check around the lounge and restaurant. She's not there, either. I go to the top-most deck and find her leaning on the rail at the front of the boat, her jet black hair blowing in the wind, and her strapless blue dress showing off her sun-kissed skin. She's a vision even from behind. If only she didn't already say I'm off limits. There's no way for me to prove I'm not everything she fears, because I am like most of the pilots she's described. I can't settle down and commit. That's why I'm here with a fake fiancée. That's why I chose this career. My life has even *less* commitment than the men she's used to. I'm not tied to a major airline. I make my own schedule and live by *my* terms. In fact, this is the most commitment I've shown in years toward any woman. It's somewhat alarming how much I haven't hated it. Regardless, I have her to myself for two days, in paradise, and I plan to make the most of it. Even if it will hurt like hell when she runs as far away from me as possible as soon as this is over.

Jolene

The ferry boat moves forward and I marvel at how incredibly beautiful the water is. I've never seen water so blue in my life. I wonder if the people who live here realize how amazing their country is? Beauty everywhere you look, fun music, amazing food, gorgeous Greek men—why am I leaving in a couple of days again? I'm not Greek, but I'm definitely considering it if this was my life every day. I'm doing it for Jimmy, so why shouldn't I do this for myself? I laugh to myself and shake my head at how silly I'm being. The sun is making me crazy, so I turn around to go back inside the boat. I come to an abrupt stop when I see Jimmy.

"What are you doing?" I ask.

His hands are in his khaki shorts pockets, and his thin white button up is unbuttoned at the top. "Watching you."

"Creeper...I knew you were a closet stalker," I say and try to fight back a smile. "I'm going to go find some water."

"We're surrounded by it. Shouldn't be too difficult."

"To drink, smart ass." I take a step, and he jumps in front of me. Raising his hand, he puts a strand of loose hair behind my ear. He's wearing sunglasses, so I can't get a read on what he's thinking.

"Jolene," he whispers. "I want you to still pretend to be mine. Even though nobody is around. Be mine these next two days, even if it's only pretend. Be mine."

I can't speak because I'd love nothing more than to be his. I hate that he uses the word 'pretend' because I'm not sure how much I'm pretending anymore. He's so sweet, spontaneous, crazy, and childish at times, but it's all part of his charm. He's a grown man running from commitment, but I'm a woman who is searching for it. We're literally running in two different directions, yet still colliding into each other. I'm terrified that he's going to take my heart and keep running. The sun shines on him as I take in his gorgeous face and sincere eyes that match the Mediterranean Sea behind him. He really believes we can share two days together and come out of it unscathed. I barely survived a passionate night in a hotel room with him on a rainy night. How am I going to survive this real-life fantasy for forty-eight hours? I'm not foolish enough to think he'll fall in love with me. That he's going to magically be ready to settle, especially for me when there's beautiful women throwing themselves at him? That and he has a life of adventure ahead of him. This is the best I'm going to get. But hey, it's more than most get. I nod, even though I'm both elated and crushed at the same time.

His lips take mine, and I wrap my arms around his neck. My hair whips around us and our bodies sway with the ship. He eases me against the wall and pins me there with his body. The wind and waves are so loud that I doubt I'd hear anyone if they stumbled upon us.

"You're mine...at least for the next two days," Jimmy says against my lips. I nod again and he squeezes me tighter against the wall and his body. "Say it to me. Tell me. I have to hear you say it, Jolene."

"I'm yours."

Jimmy's lips crash back down on mine. When we're both out of breath, he pulls back, "This is going to be the best two days of your life." He takes my hand and begins to lead me away.

That's what I'm afraid of.

CHAPTER 15

Jolene

We get settled in a little hotel that's on a beach that's not too far from the main section of town. I walk around our small room and open the balcony door. The room is tiny, but the view more than makes up for it. It's definitely hot, though, so I leave the doors open.

"Is there no air conditioning?"

Jimmy chuckles. "No. You'll find most hotels in Greece don't have air conditioning. Why would you need it when you can have fresh air from outside?"

"I don't know why I asked that, to be fair. Most of the hotels I've been to in Europe don't have air conditioning either."

Jimmy comes to stand behind me and wraps his arms around my midsection. "A lot of my aunts believe that the cold air from the air conditioning makes them sick anyway."

"My aunts believe if you don't wear socks in the winter, you'll catch your death. And you might as well sign your own death warrant if you go outside with wet hair." We both chuckle. I look over my shoulder and around him at the small bed. "Is there another room, because I only see one bed?"

Jimmy holds me tighter and speaks into my neck. "I thought we agreed that you're mine today and tomorrow. I can't exactly give you the best two days of your life if you're not with me. I'm good, but even I have my limits. And all I know is that I've reached my limits of being good in your presence." I shiver as I feel his tongue lick my skin before his lips kiss my neck. "If you're hot, maybe we should remove this."

His hands gather the bottom of my dress and pulls it up and over my head. Slowly, his fingers feather along my sides. I'm not sure what to do with my hands, because if I turn around to begin to undress him, he'll stop what he's doing. *And I don't want that.* So, I keep my hands at my side as I simply relish the feel of his own slowly making their way to my underwear. He gives them a tug, allowing them to fall to my feet. I step out and kick them to the side.

"Jo," he whispers in my ear. "Judging by the way your nipples are poking through your bra and your body is humming, I assume you want me to fuck you as bad as I am dying to fuck you. However, I'd like for it to be crystal clear." His touches are no longer featherlight, but claiming, as he slides his hands over my bra and squeezes my breasts. He moves his lips to the other side of my neck and trails open-mouthed kisses to my ear. "Tell me. I'm tired of getting myself off when I know how good you feel. How good you taste. How to make you orgasm over and over again. And to have you so close these past couple of days, *knowing* how sweet it is to be inside you and not being able to..." A sound close to a growl comes from deep in his throat.

"Shut up and fuck me already." I turn around and push him. He stumbles back toward the bed with a cocky smirk—and I'm about to wipe that smirk right off his face.

Jimmy

Seeing Jolene take charge and practically demand my dick has me feeling pretty proud of myself. That is, until she speaks.

"You know the main difference between a Greek and an American?" She reaches for my shirt and pulls it off.

"What is that?"

"You love to talk, while I want action." Leaning down, she whispers, "Now."

"Impatience is the word that comes to mind. But lucky for you, sweetheart, I'm a whole lot of *both*," I say as I undo the button to my jeans. *She wants action... boy, is she about to get it.* "Elvis had a song about–"

She places her fingers to my lips. "Don't reference an Elvis song during this moment."

"Maybe I should use my tongue in other ways to persuade you?"

Her eyes brighten at my words and her cheeks flush. Not so cocky now, are we? If I'm being honest, I'm not as self-assured either. She makes me vulnerable. She makes me feel different and doubt if I'm really

ARROGANT ARRIVAL

happy with how my life is. I'm starting to want more but I doubt if she'd take a chance on me. I have two days to make her realize that there's something real between us. Forty-eight hours to show her how much I can worship her. How good we can both be *together*. How much better life can get. So I take a page out of her book, spinning her around and pushing her onto the bed. I place a kiss on her thigh. Knowing that she wants her action *now*—her words not mine—I go straight for it. Following her directive, her order. Her back arches as I devour her. It doesn't take long for her legs to tighten around me as she crumbles at my tongue. Moaning my name as if she's praying to the heavens. Now, I'm about to show her that this Greek god is about to super-size her order. Extra-large, coming right up.

CHAPTER 16

Jolene

"Let's go get something to eat before it gets too late," I say as I slowly trail my finger along Jimmy's bare chest while curled up next to him naked in bed. My head bobs up and down as he chuckles. "What's so funny about being hungry?"

"Did you forget where we are? It's not even that late. Most people here don't eat until ten at night. We have plenty of time." He turns his head so he can look at me. "Besides, I'm not that hungry since I've already *eaten*."

"You're such a perv."

"Oh! That's not the tune you were singing earlier."

"It's not that I didn't enjoy it. I didn't say that. But you're still a pervert. And I need to keep up my energy if you plan on doing more of that."

"So, you are hungry, then?" He raises up in bed, forcing me to have to raise up as well. I wrap the sheet around me and nod. "Feeling like some meat?"

"Yeah, that sounds good."

ARROGANT ARRIVAL

"I've got some Greek sau—"

Jerking the pillow from underneath his head, I smack him as hard as I can before he can even finish that sentence. "I. Need. Food." I jump out of bed and begin getting dressed. I check my phone and see that it's five in the afternoon. *Where did the day go?* Travel and... I look over at the sexiest man I've ever met lying in bed. *Well, it was an afternoon well spent.* Jimmy rolls out of bed and stretches as he stands, completely unashamed by being completely exposed. He notices me eyeing him and winks. Correction, make that the sexiest and most arrogant man I've ever met.

Ahh, he'll do. *Barely.*

We walk outside, and instead of going to the car, I tug Jimmy's hand toward the street. "It's so nice out and there's so much to see. Let's walk."

"Fine by me." He squeezes my hand and brings it to his lips. "Hard to do that while driving a stick shift."

My heart warms a little that he loves holding and kissing my hand. Such a little gesture that's so simple yet incredibly sweet. We pass tourist shops, outside farmers' markets, and at every turn, beautiful architecture and landscaping. The sound of the bouzouki strings hum somewhere off in the distance. I watch a few kids playing soccer while their parents enjoy coffee and chatting outside. Laughter rings out from other cafés and other people walking. The culture and country is simply beautiful. Nobody seems to be in a hurry. They all are just enjoying life. I think back to me always rushing from terminal to terminal. Even when I'm not working, I'm always in and out of everywhere I go. Even relationships. This is the slowest I've ever taken life. Walking down a cobblestone street, holding hands, and simply enjoying the fresh air and life around me. That's living. For the first time in forever, I feel like I'm living my life and not rushing through it. Better yet, I'm not doing it alone.

We've been walking for a while when we come to the end of all the shops, cafés, and businesses. Jimmy looks back and asks, "See any place you want to try? We'd need the car to go any farther. Looks like mostly farmland from here on out, and then it'll be the next town. Which we can go, I'd just prefer not by foot."

"There was a place...I can't pronounce the name, but I remember where it was."

"Lead the way, gorgeous."

"What a twist, now I'm leading you around Greece. Are we on equal footing here?"

Jimmy laughs and pulls me into him, my back to his chest. With his arms holding me tight, he whispers into my ear. "We are nowhere near being on equal footing."

"Oh, really? And how do you figure that? What, because you speak the language? Most people here speak English."

"We are not on equal footing because how can a simple man such as myself be equal to such a beautiful goddess."

I bite back my reply and hate myself for loving such a cheesy line. "You are so full of it, Dimitrios Georgakopolous."

ARROGANT ARRIVAL

With a heavy Greek accent, Jimmy speaks between kisses on my neck, "You are the goddess of the sky. I worship your spirit," *kiss* and then he moves up, "your fire," *kiss* right below my ear, "your body," and then he growls into my ear, "and most of all, the taste of your heavenly sweet cu–"

"Whoa!" I pull away, looking around frantically. "There are children around."

"Tsk. Tsk. Where is your head? I was going to say *cunning* mind."

I roll my eyes as he stands there looking devilishly handsome with a wicked grin. We go back to walking, and easily find the little restaurant I'd spotted. There's outside seating with twinkling lights strung from the surrounding trees even though it's not dark out yet. It's a very romantic and intimate little spot. I point and say, "Here." Jimmy smiles and leads us to a small little table for two in a corner. I look out to the ocean and listen to the gentle waves.

"You chose a very romantic place. But I'll go ahead and break the news to you…I'm a sure thing."

I roll my eyes at him again, and then sigh. "I think everywhere here is romantic. Look at this place. In fact, you're the one who suggested we go to an island, just the two of us. But I'll go ahead and tell you, I'm *not* a sure thing. So you might want to up your game, buddy."

Before he can give one of his cocky remarks, our waiter arrives. Jim speaks to him in Greek and the waiter hands us our menus with a single nod and leaves. Thankfully, the menu is written in Greek and English. I'm starving, so everything sounds appetizing. I decide to go with the tou tou makia, a chicken with noodles and a red tomato sauce. The waiter returns with wine. As he pours our glasses, I raise an eyebrow at Jimmy who is looking smug. His facial expression clearly reads *challenge accepted.* I was only teasing him. I am definitely a for-sure thing for him while we are here, even if my heart won't survive it. I thought we'd already established this. Obviously an afternoon spent in bed was a sure sign that he didn't have to try too hard with me. Either way, I'm excited to see what he has up his sleeve. I take a sip of my wine while Jimmy tells the waiter our order in Greek.

As the waiter walks away, Jim makes a dramatic display of picking up his napkin and placing it in his lap as he keeps his eyes focused on me. "Do you have a bucket list while here in Greece? Especially while we're away from all the others."

I take another sip of wine and then smile at him over the cup. "I think—" All kinds of touristy things are on the tip of my tongue, but I stop and look out into the ocean again. The waves are calming. Fewer and smaller waves hit the shore now. Even the ocean that's always moving slows down from time to time. "Relax."

"Okay, I am." He tilts his head toward me, "Believe me, anything you say I'll probably be game for. Don't worry. Tell me."

I giggle. "Not you relax. That's what I want to do. I just want to relax. No plans and absolutely no schedule. I want to take everything slow and easy."

"Done. The rest of the night will be spent in leisure, and tomorrow we'll take the day as it comes." He holds up his wine glass and waits for me. I take mine and hold it up. We clink our glasses together and drink on it.

ARROGANT ARRIVAL

"That sounds absolutely perfect."

Our tomato and cucumber salads arrive, along with some olives and bread. As we eat, music plays over the speakers and my body involuntarily sways. I don't even realize I'm doing it until I catch Jimmy watching me. He tosses his napkin on the table and stands, holding his hand out to me with a smirk.

"Um, nobody is dancing?" I mumble, refusing to take his hand.

"That's their misfortune." He gestures with his fingers for me to stand.

"Jimmy, sit down. Don't you have any pride?"

He tosses his head back and laughs. When he begins shaking his head, I know I'm in trouble. The music changes to an upbeat melody. Jim's hips sway as he brings his arms up, snapping his fingers.

The waiter comes walking quickly over to us. I want to cover my head. We're about to get kicked out, and that's pretty damn hard to do seeing as we're already outside. Jimmy continues to dance, completely oblivious to the waiter. I try to warn him by discreetly pointing to look behind him. But then the waiter arrives and shouts, "OPA!" He claps, and then to my surprise, literally kicks his foot back and slaps the heel of his shoe. He falls into dancing with Jimmy. I look around, trying to figure out when I fell into some Greek musical.

Jimmy turns to me, and judging by the look in his eyes, I know I'm in for it. He begins swaying his hips more slowly, and suggestive. He makes his way closer to my chair. This is payback for when I danced for him. His blue-green eyes have gone dark, and a few black strands of his hair fall forward into his eyes. A few people stop and watch, and it's easy to spot the tourists from the Greeks. Mostly because one set gawks and has their phones up, while the other set are clapping and snapping their fingers to the beat of the music. Jimmy begins to slowly ease back from me. The song is coming to an end, so he turns to the onlookers. He sings part of the words of the song very loudly and then does a spin and kick. He holds his arms out and dramatically bows. Everyone laughs and claps. What a showman he is.

I shake my head at him as he sits back down. "Unbelievable."

"Believe it, sweetheart." He takes a big drink of his wine. "And believe that before this trip is over, I'm going to have you out there dancing and turning tricks in the street."

"That makes me sound like a hooker."

"Fine, I'll have you dancing on top of the tables."

"Not better."

"Oh, I know a club where you can get on stage with the singer and we throw rose petals on you while you dance."

"You want me to dance on stage now? At least that sounds more legit." My voice drips with sarcasm. "Instead of flowers, can you throw money at me, instead?"

Jimmy chuckles. "We only do that at parties."

"What?"

"At parties. You know engagement parties, weddings, baptisms... While everyone dances, we throw money and it helps pay for the band."

ARROGANT ARRIVAL

"Really? I was only joking, but now that sounds kind of fun. I'll dance and you can make it rain singles on me. I'm really loving this Greek living."

"Don't be silly. I'd at least throw a few fives in."

We both laugh as our waiter brings our food to the table. The food smells delicious. I immediately dig in. The flavoring is incredible. It's so cheesy, and the tomato-based sauce has just the right amount of seasoning. The chicken is so tender, and the little square pasta noodles are al dente. I eat bite after bite. I finally come up for air to get a sip of wine when I meet Jimmy's amused eyes. He reaches over with his napkin and wipes my chin.

"I was going to ask to try a bite since it seems so scrumptious, but was afraid I might get bitten."

I chuckle, "Don't act like that's what stopped you. Because you and I both know you like it when I sink my teeth into you." I go to swat his hand, but at the last minute think better of it. I grab his hand and lightly bite his finger before wrapping my lips around it and gently sucking. His eyes darken, and with a pop, I pull his finger out. Jimmy takes his finger and places it on his tongue. My eyes are fascinated by how his tongue licks his finger, and then his lips wrap around the digit. His voice lowers as he says, "That is scrumptious. No wonder you ate every last bite."

I slide my plate toward him and smirk. "You're welcome to lick the plate clean."

"I'd rather lick something else—"

"Um...excuse me." My eyes widen in horror as a new waiter has come to our table. We both turn to the gentleman standing there holding a bottle of wine.

"Compliments of the older couple over there." He nods toward his right. We look over to see an elderly couple wave at us.

Jimmy smiles and waves to them as he asks the waiter, "Why?"

The waiter smiles and shrugs. He speaks in Greek and then Jimmy chuckles. He turns to the couple and places his hands together and lightly bows. He turns to me and translates as the waiter leaves. "They said we remind them of when they were young. They said something about young love. Congratulations. And to enjoy."

I wave to the couple and call out 'thank you' in butchered Greek. "Efcharistó"

They stand and wave bye to us as they slowly walk away. Jimmy pours me another glass of wine. "Well, I guess we know how we're spending our night. *Drunk.*"

"We could share it?"

"Were you not planning to share it with me?"

"With other guests. I'm going to be tipsy if I drink much more."

We each pour ourselves a glass, and then Jim looks to the table closest to us. He asks in Greek if they'd like a glass. Another table close to us I hear speaking in English, so I ask if they'd like a glass. We pour them a glass. All the tables surrounding us laugh and drink. Jimmy pours me another glass, and I am starting to feel the effects of the wine. An upbeat song comes over the speakers and Jimmy grins. He stands and once again starts dancing. Easing his way around the table, he leans down into my ear and purrs, "Come dance with me."

ARROGANT ARRIVAL

Laughing, I shake my head. "I don't dance in public, and I'm more than likely going to trip as I'm slightly inebriated."

"Come on, you danced just fine in front of my family."

"That wasn't in *public*. And I might've been a little..." I shake my shoulders and smile at him.

He raises his eyebrows and extends his arms. "This is like family. This is a family of people all wanting to have a good time." They raise their glasses to him. He looks back to me and smirks. "Come dance with me... chicken."

"Chicken?"

He leans into my ear and whispers. "Chicken."

I turn up my glass and down my wine. Before I can think better of it, I stand and push his shoulder, moving him out of my way. Then, I dance.

Like no one is watching.

When in reality, Jimmy is watching my every move.

CHAPTER 17

Jimmy

The night is going better than I could have ever imagined. I'm having more fun than I can ever remember having. I don't know what it is about Jolene, but I live to surprise her. I love seeing that shocked look in her eyes when I do something crazy or embarrassing. Honestly, I typically don't act this bold, but there's something about her that brings it out in me.

Her smile. That's what it is. Seeing it makes my chest swell, and that light in her eyes when she looks at me, knowing that I did that. It usually makes an appearance when I'm making a complete ass of myself, but nevertheless, I put that look of happiness on her face.

I was determined to get her to let loose and dance, and here she is, belly dancing on an island in an outdoor restaurant by the beach. Her sweet laugh is music to my ears as she says, "Nobody else is dancing."

"So? I don't care about anybody else." I reach out

ARROGANT ARRIVAL

and grab her hips and pull her against my front. "I don't want to dance with them."

She turns around, and the smirk on face her radiates more sinful promises, "I feel like taking this dance somewhere more private. What about you?"

"You most definitely don't have to ask me twice, koritsi mou."

We step off the wood flooring of the restaurant and onto the rocks and pebbles of the beach. We can still hear the music, so Jolene continues to dance as we walk. She's so incredibly sexy, and it blows my mind how I don't think she really knows how special she is. Suddenly, she stops and turns to me with a look of horror.

I reach out to her and ask, "Hey, what's wrong?"

"Nothing, but is there a restroom nearby?"

I look around. "There's a few tourist shops and cafés up there. Let's go see. Are you okay?"

"Yeah, yeah. Let's go."

"If you need to throw up, nobody is around. There's some bushes over there."

Her eyes widen and she shakes her head. "No, no. I need a restroom. Not a bush."

I lead her up the hill from the beach and back to the sidewalk. We walk along the shops and come to a relatively large one. "Want a magnet?"

"What?" She pants as her face looks like she's almost in physical pain.

"We have to buy something before we just use their restroom. It's not really acceptable to go in a place only to use their restroom."

"Fine. Sure. Grab anything."

I pick up a little magnet and ask the gentleman at the counter if he has a restroom Jolene can use. He points to a door in the back. Jolene rushes back and runs in the little room. However, as soon as the door closes, it reopens.

She comes up to me and whispers. "There's no toilet. Only a sink and ... a hole."

I nod. "Yeah, a lot of bathrooms in Greece don't use the full toilet."

She raises her hands up and looks to be on the verge of tears. "Jimmy, there's *no* toilet. Not even part of one, like the bowl." She leans closer and grits out, "I can't go in a hole."

I nod, "Okay. Let's try the café."

I tell the gentleman thank you and leave with our magnet. We go to the café, and I purchase a bottle of water. Jolene rushes to their restroom and five seconds later walks past me and out of the café.

Catching up to her, I ask, "What happened?"

"They had stalls and bowls but no *seats*. I was scared I'd fall in. And the doors on the stalls were like textured glass. The kind you can't completely see through – but *you can see*. Jimmy, I have to go! And I need a full bathroom with privacy! Why is this such a struggle?"

"I'm sorry, sweetheart. Here in Greece, public restrooms aren't a big thing. Can you make it a little longer? Let's try this place."

Jolene groans and I hear her stomach gurgle. She looks like she's on the verge of tears, and before I can ask again, she takes off in a sprint. I chase after her.

ARROGANT ARRIVAL

"I'm going back to the room!" she calls back. "I know it for sure has a bathroom. I can't keep hunting. I have to go!"

By the time we get to the room, I'm exhausted and sweating. Jolene rushes to the bathroom and slams the door shut, locking it. I hear...well, I hear what I would have only assumed was a man on the other side of the door had I not seen her run in there with my own eyes.

"For the love of God, turn on the television! Turn the volume up *loud*! Please!"

"Jo," I try to hide the smile in my voice and hold back laughter. "Honey, sweetheart." I have to bite my hand to keep from laughing because I hear her passing gas—*loudly*. "Are you okay?"

"No," she cries out followed by more sounds. "Please, go away! This is humiliating enough as it is!"

"Jo, babe, everyone has these types of issues at some point in their life." I stifle a laugh. "And everyone gets diarrhea and passes gas." The more noises she makes, the more I want to die laughing. I gather my composure before continuing. "It's natural."

"This is not natural! I don't know what I ate or drank, but never a–again." Her voice is strained, followed by more unpleasant sounds and then she yells. "Will you please give me some privacy! Get away from the door! Take a walk!"

Snickering, I walk over to the television and turn it on. I turn up the volume, and I faintly hear Jolene yell, "Thank you!"

Even over the television, I can still hear her rumblings, but I won't ever tell her that.

Jolene

Having the worst case of gastrointestinal issues is a sure way to win any man over, right? This is hands down the most mortifying moment of my life. I'd rather fall down the stairs and flash his family my ass again than this. Should I even come out of the bathroom? I don't know how much longer I can remain trapped in here with the smell. Oh, my God. The smell. Why couldn't there be a window in here? This room is so small, we are going to smell this all night long. Fuck. My. Life. I ease the door open just enough for me to slide through and quickly close the door behind me in hopes of not releasing the smell into the room.

Jim is lying on the bed in only black briefs watching television. His sculpted abs are on display. His dark hair is messy, making him look sexier than should be legal. Those blue eyes that rival the blue of the Mediterranean Sea sparkle at me. And that smile that would make any red-blooded human drop their pants is turned up to full panty-melting mode. *Great. This gorgeous man just heard me fart...several times.* It could've happened to anyone. It's probably happened to him. I hold my head up high as I make my way to my suitcase for absolutely nothing other than to get out of making eye contact.

"Jo."

"Yes?" My voice comes out high.

"*Jo.*"

ARROGANT ARRIVAL

I sigh and turn around to face him. He stares at me with serious eyes and not a trace of a smile on his face now. Then, he lifts his leg up and farts. Slowly, he lays his leg back down and stares at me. I burst out laughing, but he doesn't even crack a smile. I walk over to the bed and place my hands on my hips. "Was that just for me?"

"I've been holding it until you came out."

"That must've been painful."

"You have no idea. I had to turn the tv up louder to mute my cries of gas pain."

Taking my hand, Jimmy kisses the knuckles, and then in a voice of mock seriousness says, "I'd endure any pain for you. Anything. I'd birth a child for you if you needed me to. But you don't have to torture me. Can you go open the balcony door? Some of the smell is seeping from the bathroom." My jaw drops, and Jimmy bursts out laughing. He pulls me down on top of him and holds me to him. "Just so you know, this has been the most romantic night I've ever experienced."

"It started out romantic with dancing under the stars by the ocean, but I don't think hearing me in the bathroom was a recipe for pure romance."

"That's just us being open and comfortable with each other."

"No, that's because I was beyond uncomfortable that I was forced to endure that. You should've left the room!"

"Besides what we've just lived through the past twenty minutes, did you enjoy the rest of the night?"

"Sadly, this was the most romantic night for me, too." We take a moment to simply gaze into each other's eyes. Then, Jimmy brings his lips to mine. He rolls us over to where he is on top of me. I suck my lips under my teeth and then whisper, "Even after all that, you still want to…"

"Are you kidding? You're so gorgeous and incredibly sexy." He begins removing my clothes and then growls, "Besides, in all honestly I'm impressed with what you were packing. You're a real woman. There was none of those pansy little airy toots. You farted like a beast."

"Stop! I'm going to die."

"You most certainly are going to think that because I'm about to take you to heaven."

I bring my hand to Jim's cheek and, while looking into his gorgeous blue-green eyes, ask "The cheesiness. You're something else. What am I going to do with you, Jimmy?"

"Anything you want. Just don't leave me too broken."

CHAPTER 18
Jolene

The next morning, I'm surprised when I wake up and Jimmy isn't in bed. I go ahead and shower and then get dressed. When I walk out of the bathroom, Jimmy is back in the room like he'd never been gone.

"Good morning," he comes up and kisses me on the forehead. "What do you say to exploring some of the island? There's a cave I want you to see. We can take a boat ride through it. But we have to be there by noon to get the full effect. Also, I was thinking ice cream on the beach?"

"That sounds fantastic!"

"Great! Let's get going."

We walk outside and Jimmy goes to a four-wheeler. "Hop on!"

"Why did you get this?"

"Well, you can't see as much with the car, and it is nice out. But then I thought, what if we had any issues and needed to get back to the room quickly? So, your carriage awaits."

Too moved by his thoughtfulness to be embarrassed, I walk over and wrap my arms around his neck. "You know, you can be pretty charming when you want to be."

"For a pilot?"

The comment makes me flinch a little. He's right, though. I've been a little ridiculous on my prejudice toward pilots. He waits for my response, and I honestly don't know what to say. Instead, I smile and nod. Play it flirty. "Less arrogant looks pretty damn good on you."

"Yeah, I know... Keep hanging around. I might surprise you some more."

The first place Jimmy drives us to is the Melissani Cave. We hop off the four-wheeler and Jimmy gets in line to purchase our tickets. There's a little awning set up that already has a few people waiting to buy tickets, but luckily, the line is moving quickly. We follow the others down a dark and cold stairway. Little boats are lined up, but they don't look real...they actually look like they have been photoshopped on the water, like they're floating above it. The water is so incredibly blue and clear. It's like nothing I've ever seen before. I reach my hand out and touch a rock and it's so cold. I wasn't expecting that. We hop in the boat and I stare, fascinated, at how gorgeous the turquoise-blue water is. The guy paddling our boat says the water is very deep, around twenty to thirty meters. It's crazy because I can clearly see the stones at the bottom because the water is so incredibly clear, like if reached into the water I could touch each and every one of them.

"This has to be the clearest water in the world. It's beyond words beautiful," I whisper to Jimmy as I

ARROGANT ARRIVAL

am in awe looking around the cave. The sun begins to move and shine through the opening above us. "I'm so grateful you chose this to do today. Thank you." He just smiles at me, clearly satisfied with his choice.

"Right on time," Jimmy says to me. The light from the sun shines through the opening above us and into the water. The water sparkles and reflects and shines on the walls of the cave. My God, I gasp at how magical it is. Our boat goes a little farther in, and then it gets darker in the cave. It's a little spooky and a lot cold. The boat finally comes back around to the opening above us where we were picked up. As we come back into the light with the sun shining bright above us, I'm curious about the water temperature. Discreetly, I reach over the boat and quickly dip the tips of my fingers in. Jimmy is watching me.

"Holy hell, it's ice cold," I tell him.

He searches my eyes and gives me a small smile. "Isn't it amazing how something can be so stunningly beautiful and look so incredibly inviting, but really, underneath it all, it is impossible to touch and so very dangerous."

"What?"

"You'll only get hurt in here."

The way Jimmy's eyes study me, I don't think he's talking about the cave or the water.

Jimmy

As she wraps her arms around me and I start the four-wheeler, I want to kick myself. I'm falling hard for

Jolene. I wanted two days to show her I was genuine. But she doesn't want a relationship with me. She shouldn't want anything to do with me. And honestly, I shouldn't want more either. This is all fake. I asked her to be mine for this trip, so how can I believe the warm and inviting look in her eyes right now? She made it clear the first time we met that we had no future...and even the second time we met she said in no uncertain terms that she doesn't want me. Well, except for sex. I feel like such a fool. Why am I getting upset over this? I have a beautiful woman's arm wrapped around me and I'm pouting because I'm wanting more from her. More than what she's willing to give. I've never wanted more. With anyone. Leave it to me to run off and pick the one woman who hates pilots. I only love three things in my life: my family, flying, and Greece. Jolene fits perfectly into my entire world, well, except the fact that she despises my career. I'm not a passenger in life, though—I'm the pilot. That's part of who I am.

I zoom through the winding roads to try and clear my head before we stop again. I don't want to ruin our last day together. There's a beach that's kind of isolated, so off the beaten path that it's remained clean and beautiful, so I begin heading in that direction. Right before coming to the turn that leads to the zig-zagging road down a mountain, I stop at the side of the road and point in the direction of where we are heading.

"That's where we are going. Down there."

Jolene squeezes me tighter and squeals. "Oh my gosh, it's stunning. I've never seen water so blue. I know I keep saying that, but each time the water is more stunning and gorgeous. I can't wait. Although, getting down there is going to make us dizzy, it looks like."

I chuckle. The road is a clear zig-zag going down the mountain. There's an ice cream stand across the street from us. "Let's grab a cone and head down. Do you care to hold mine while I drive?"

"I'll gladly hold your cone."

I turn around and grin at Jolene, who is looking absolutely adorable in her little pink helmet. "Did you just make a dirty joke?"

"You're rubbing off on me. Wait—I left myself open for that one...don't say anything. Let's just go get our ice cream."

I can't stop the huge smile from spreading across my face. Once I'm off the four-wheeler, I lift Jolene. She yelps and wraps her legs around me. Everything's so perfect right now. I'm holding the most beautiful physically and spirited woman in my arms with her legs wrapped around me, standing on top of the world with one of the most gorgeous beaches in the world below us. I don't want to leave this island and go back to reality.

We both get vanilla cones as I throw one last comment out to Jolene about me being anything but vanilla, and I begin driving us slowly down the mountain. The pace is so slow that she doesn't need to hold on to me, which is good since both of her hands are holding ice cream cones.

We reach the bottom of the mountain and I park the four-wheeler. There's only a few other cars here, thankfully, so we'll have the place practically to ourselves. I hop off, and remove my shirt. Jolene hands me my ice cream cone. Instead of taking it, I grab her wrist and then lick a drip of vanilla off her finger. Her eyes darken and I love knowing I'm affecting her just as much as she is me.

I place my hands on her waist and begin walking her toward the coves in the cliffs. The waves crash against the rocks and I feel the mist against my legs. Jolene is still holding my ice cream cone and brings it to her lips. My blood pumps faster as her mouth opens and her tongue licks around the cone's perimeter before her mouth closes over the white cream.

"Koritsi mou." I barely manage to say. "I'm ready for a taste."

My tongue slides across her lips, licking the sweet cream. I take her wrist again and lick each finger that has melted vanilla. "It's about to get messy. Maybe you should remove your clothes."

I take the cones from her. She throws me a flirty smile as she looks at me from under long lashes. She removes her top and shorts, wearing only a bikini now. She reaches for the cones but I raise them up, out of her reach. "I'm not finished," she pouts.

"I couldn't agree more. You're not. Go ahead and finish."

"Wait – what? I'm not getting nude."

Pretending to give her the cone, I hold it toward her, but then dab it between her chest. "Opa. I'm sorry. Here, I'll clean it up." My tongue slides between her breasts.

"I could go in the water to clean up."

"I was taught to clean up my messes. Besides, something this sweet shouldn't be wasted." I take the

ARROGANT ARRIVAL

cone and then dribble more ice cream over chest and down her slender neck. Licking and sucking as I go.

"Were you also taught to share?" She takes the other cone and holds it above my shoulder, allowing the melting ice cream to trail down my body. The sight of her tongue peeking out between those full lips is the most erotic thing I've ever witnessed.

Somewhere between us taking turns licking each other, our cones become soggy. Jolene bursts into a fit of giggles when hers starts to break.

"You're holding it too tight." I stare at the poor cone as ice cream squishes out.

"You've never complained before."

"Ooh. Haven't you turned into a dirty girl?" Her reply is to giggle and shove the remnants of the cone into my chin. "You're going to pay for that."

She squeals and takes off running. I chase her through the cove as waves splash against our shins. I wrap my arms around her waist and tackle her to me. Her laughing immediately stops when I sink into the shallow water with her on my lap. The waves push her body forward and then pull her back, while I encourage and welcome the pleasant friction. I claim her mouth and greedily take everything she is willing to give. Mists of water from the waves spray on us as the sea continues to pushes and pull us. As I kiss along her neck I taste the sugar from the ice cream, the salt from the sea, and the taste that is uniquely her. The combined flavors are fucking addicting and my taste buds can't get enough.

Jolene reaches between us and lowers my swim trunks. I slide them off with one hand and toss them back on to the rocks. Next I pull her top strings loose and toss them, as well as her bottoms, to the rocks. I anchor Jolene firmly to me as I dive into her.

When we both come apart in each other's arms and catch our breath, Jolene looks down. "Remind me to watch what I say around you. Every time I say I'm not going to do something, you seem determined to make it happen." She blushes and looks around. The people are far away from us and we're in the water hidden within the coves. "Where's my top and bottom?"

I look back and easily spot her turquoise top and bottom. It's my shorts that I'm now worried about. Jolene swims farther out into the water and remains hunkered down while I hurry to grab her bikini. I swim out to her and search for my trunks. Jolene giggles as she gets dressed.

"Where the hell could they have gone? I saw them land on the rocks."

"Maybe a big wave came in?"

I can't help but give her a cocky smile. "Baby, we created some big waves."

"I hope you don't find your shorts." She snorts. "And since you just wore your swimming trunks as shorts today, what are you going to do? You only have a shirt."

"I know you'd love nothing more than for me to walk around naked all day, but that wouldn't be fair to every other man out there. I'm a humble guy, and really try not to brag."

I then notice a soggy ice cream cone floating by, or what's left of one. And not far from it is a pair of black swim trunks. I quickly begin swimming toward the trunks. Of course, a wave would have to come at that moment. The wave crashes on top of me and pulls me and my shorts farther out to sea. I try to swim faster to compete with the next wave that's about to come in. I'm close to my shorts when a jet ski comes zipping by. It's an older man and woman riding it. They're wearing sunglasses, so I can't make out their expressions. They stop by my shorts and pick them up.

"Thank you," I call out.

The woman blushes and looks away. The guy nods and hands me my shorts wordlessly. Yeah, he knew exactly how my shorts disappeared based on him looking over and seeing Jo in the water still. It's guy code as he smirks at me before driving off. Quickly, I slide them on and swim back to Jolene. After our intense lovemaking and my marathon swim, I'm exhausted. We go over to the beach and sit down on the ground. I wrap my arm around her shoulders and she lies her head against me.

"Let's stay here until sunset," she whispers.

"Anything for you, koritsi mou."

CHAPTER 19
Jolene

We get back to the hotel and shower together. Jim said he was tired, but that didn't seem to slow him down any. Which if he wasn't exhausted before, I know he is now. Once we've finished, Jimmy and I hop in the car to go out for dinner. I'm dressed in a clingy black shimmer dress that covers only one shoulder and has a small slit on the side. My hair hangs loose with big flowy silk curls. I feel sexy and carefree on our last night together.

I feel heat from his strong hand on the small of my back as he leads me into the upscale, yet modern restaurant. A hostess leads us to our table.

"What do you think of this place?" Jimmy asks while looking over the menu.

"It's very classy and beautiful. But I think the little place we went to last night was my favorite. It was so unique and ...well, Greek. You can't find places like that back home."

ARROGANT ARRIVAL

Jimmy nods in agreement and closes his menu. "You want Greek culture dining?"

I look around the restaurant. "I mean, this is a Greek restaurant and we're in Greece."

"No, no. You like the music and authentic food?" I smile and nod. "Then what are we doing? Get up. I've got just the place in mind."

I smile as I follow him out of the restaurant and to the car. We go past all the markets and hotels to a more secluded area of the island. Off in the distance, I can see lights shining up into the night sky. I know we've arrived at our destination by the distant sound of music and cars scattered about. Jimmy parks the car on the side of the road behind an already long line of cars and motorcycles. When I open the car door, I can already hear loud music and people cheering. It sounds like a concert. I look up and see the same bright lights moving around, lighting up the night sky.

"Where are we going? I thought we were going to eat."

"I could tell you, but it's one of those places you just have to *experience*. Come on, koritsi mou."

I plant my feet in the ground and pull back on his hand. "Jimmy?"

"Yeah?"

"You keep calling me that – *kor-itsy mou*. What does it mean?"

His tongue slides out and wets his lips. It's dark out here, but there's enough light from the arena and moon to make out his features. *He's nervous.* But why? I've gathered that *mou* means my. Oh gosh, what has he been calling me?

Jimmy starts to speak but then clears his throat. His eyes bore into mine as he says, "*Koritsi mou* means 'my girl.' It's not necessarily a romantic term in Greek, but...you're the only one..." He bites his bottom lip and slowly releases it. "I've never used that term on anyone but you. It feels right calling you that."

The smile that spreads across my face actually hurts. Heat pools in my belly. The term is so simple but I can tell it means a lot to him. Jim begins to fidget and appear visibly antsy.

"This is getting awkward. Let's go have fun." I hate that he downplayed our moment. I saw something in his eyes. I don't want to get my hopes up, but there was vulnerability and something else...*love?* No. I'm being foolish again.

Jimmy

We enter the gates of *Oloi Nychta*. Two guys check our I.D. and then we move forward to a building with little wooden shutters. The ticket window also has shutters on either side. I give the lady at the counter my credit card and tell them I want the VIP seating with a bottle of wine, an extra basket of flower petals, and two entrees. The woman nods and says, "Bravo." She hands me back my card along with our tickets. I place my hand on the small of Jolene's back and guide her to an archway that leads to a small entryway that's somewhat like a tunnel. When we exit, we're in an open venue surrounded by what looks like houses from little villages, all with different color window shutters and balconies. There's a curved stage on the far right, and on the far left is what looks to be a huge balcony with a white grand piano. There are steps for each house, and tables and chairs cover the rest in between. People are already filling the seats, and some who didn't purchase tickets for dining sit on the steps and stoops, or stand around.

"We're down here," I indicate to the nicer tables closer to the stage. They're not as crowded together, and there's no stoops nearby. We take our seat right as a spotlight shines on a balcony above us. A woman in a dazzling red dress steps out holding a microphone. When she begins singing, Jolene turns to me with a bright smile.

"This is amazing! What's this place called?"

"All night. Oloi Nychta. It opens at eight and stays open until five in the morning."

"Wow. Are people going to pop out of every balcony?"

"Not all. Or they might, I'm not sure. Every show is different. They only have these on certain nights each week. We just got lucky. Most performers will be on the stage. We'll get baskets of rose petals to throw as they sing and dance."

"No money?" Jolene raises an eyebrow.

"Not this time. But I can take you to one of those shows next time..." What am I saying? Will there be a next time? Jolene doesn't seem to miss my slip up.

She giggles and cuts her eyes to me. "The night's young. Who knows?"

They bring our drinks, along with a shot of ouzo. "I can drink to that." I hold up my shot glass and tip it toward her. "The night is young, kortisi mou."

"The night is definitely young."

We clink glasses and down our shots. Jolene makes a face as she forces herself to swallow the ouzo.

"That stuff tastes like liquorish and lighter fluid." She slams the glass down.

"Here's something a little sweeter and will go down much easier." I pour her a glass of wine. Our fingers touch as she accepts the glass, and I'm amazed at how every time I touch her, I get a rush. Even the slightest touches. She doesn't move her hand away, and I don't let go of the glass. I stare into her big, honey-colored eyes. The light changes in the arena then, and the spotlight shines on the stage next to us. Jolene takes her glass to redirect her attention to the stage that's filled with a full band, and now a man in tight pants and a blue shirt.

Most of the women cheer and begin to clap as he sings. Jolene cheers and sways to the music. He begins to sing the chorus of the song, and then I recognize who he is, Kostas Dalaras. He's an up-and-coming big Greek singer. He just had two big songs come out and most of the women are starstruck watching him.

Kostas is younger than me, and a huge success with his women fans of all ages. He has messy black hair, bright blue eyes, the classic Greek nose, and keeps himself very fit. Actually, there's not much difference between us, but for some reason women are going crazy over this guy. Unfortunately, it seems he just gained another new fan.

ARROGANT ARRIVAL

"He's amazing! I don't know what he's saying, but I don't want him to stop. I love this music."

"His name is Kostas. He's new, but becoming increasingly popular around the country."

"Well, now he has an American fan. So he can officially say he's famous worldwide."

I hand her the basket of pink and white flower petals. "Throw these at him then."

Jolene takes the basket and stands to get closer to the stage. Before I can tell her she's only supposed to toss a handful, she rears her hand back and the basket slips from her fingers. I burst out laughing as her hands come to her mouth, and her eyes are wide with horror. Kostas picks up the basket that just hit his shin. He stops singing and laughs.

I watch as he walks over to the edge of the stage where Jolene is standing. He crouches down and asks her in Greek what her name is through the microphone. Her full lips pout as she shakes her head and tosses her hands up. I lean forward and yell out to him her name and that she's American and doesn't speak Greek. Kostas smiles and nods. He extends his hand and speaks directly to her in Greek that she's very beautiful and welcomes her to Greece. His head turns to me and he nods toward her.

"He says you're beautiful and welcome to Greece."

Jolene smiles widely and nods. I frown as I notice she's clearly blushing. Kostas looks at her as he asks her in Greek if she came all this way just to throw a basket at him. The crowd, of course, erupts in laughter. Jolene turns to me and I translate for her. She giggles like a schoolgirl, and I'm almost ready to throw up. I was really starting to like this guy up until this point.

He asks her what brings her to Greece. I smile smugly at him as he turns to me to translate. "He wants to know why you're here?"

"I'm here on vacation with my friend," Jolene smiles at him and bats her eyelashes.

Her friend, eh? Kostas turns to me for the translation. I oblige, of course, adding my own spin to what she said and tell him in Greek, "She's here with me, her fiancé. We're celebrating our engagement."

Kostas beams at me and tells me congratulations. He reaches down and Jolene hands him her hand. He kisses her knuckles and then shakes her hand with both of his. He wishes us many years of happiness and good health. He stands and calls out into the microphone for everyone to congratulate us. "Bravo!" he cheers before erupting into song.

Jolene smiles and waves to the audience as she takes her seat. "What are they cheering so loudly for? What did he say?"

"Everyone is welcoming you to Greece. They wish you much happiness and good health."

"That was so embarrassing, but turned out to be so fun! Thank you, Jimmy. I'd have never known what he was saying if not for you translating."

"My pleasure." And then mumble to myself, "I wouldn't have had it any other way."

If she only knew what I told him, she'd probably wallop me over the head. I mean, technically, she is mine these next couple of days, and she did agree to be my fiancée—even if it is a fake one.

ARROGANT ARRIVAL

"No, I mean...everything. This vacation has turned out to be the best thing to ever happen to me. I – I just really want you to know that no matter what else happens, I'm really grateful."

I reach across the table and take her hand. "Me too."

We release our hands as the waitress places a new basket of flower petals down. We look over and Kostas winks at us before he leaves the stage. Another singer comes on stage next, and a new song begins. A few of the members of the audience go on stage and begin Greek dancing in half circles.

"We can do that?" Jolene asks.

"They allow it, but not always for the bigger performers. It depends. But most of the time people dance at their tables or on stage."

Just then, our plates are brought out and we begin to eat our chicken and potatoes. I decided we better go with something safe and easy on Jolene's stomach after last night's debacle. I want this to be the best night she has, not only on this trip but for years to come. I've resigned myself to the fact that we'll go our separate ways soon. So when she moves on to another guy, I don't want her to be able to move on from this moment. I want her to always remember me and how we felt on this night *together*.

CHAPTER 20

Jolene

I spin around as flower petals rain down on me. I laugh as I dance with people I'll probably never see again, but will certainly not forget no matter how much I drink tonight. Jimmy sits in his seat watching me on stage make a huge fool of myself. I don't care. I love Greek life, so much so that now I wish it all wasn't a lie. I wish I was here as Jimmy's girl—his koritsi. The spotlight goes off the stage to the balcony on the far side with the white grand piano. Sitting there is Kostas in all black playing the piano. I'm pretty sure my ovaries just exploded at the sight of him. I go to step off the stage, but my legs wobble. Jimmy rolls his eyes and comes to stand in front of the stage. He extends his arms, "Jump."

"Are you crazy? I'll go to the stairs."

"Nonsense. Jump. I'll catch you."

The lights go off on the stage and it's pitch black. Deciding I'll most likely break my neck trying to go down the steps, I shuffle my feet until I feel the edge of the stage. I reach in the darkness and feel Jimmy's strong hands. I jump and he wraps his arms around me in a firm hold.

"By the way, this is the only Greek you need to be ogling over." He growls in my ear. He presses my back against the side of the stage then. I suck in a breath and he must hear me, because he says, "That's better."

His hands begin to ease down my sides until he comes to the hem of my dress. He slides a hand under the tight fabric. I tighten my legs together. "Jimmy," I sigh. "Somebody will see us."

"It's pitch black in here. We have a good three minutes until the song changes. I can make you sing in that amount of time." He wastes no time sliding my panties to the side and inserting two fingers. The wrongness of us making out on the side of the stage in front of everyone, even if it is in the dark, while Kostas plays a sensual ballad is intoxicating. This is by far the kinkiest thing I've ever done, and I'm even a member of the mile high club!

Jimmy sucks on my neck as his fingers caress my most tender of areas. I grab a handful of his hair and pull him closer to me. "Jimmy. *Jimmy.*"

"That's it, koritsi mou, that's it." Him calling me that has me coming undone. "Yes," he growls into my ear as his fingers work faster. He applies the perfect amount of pressure with his thumb as he inserts two fingers. I'm about to scream out when his lips take mine. His mouth covers my moans as I ride out my orgasm on his hand. The song comes to an end and Jimmy eases his hand out from under my dress. The spotlight shines back on the stage, illuminating Jimmy's face with his messed-up black hair falling in his eyes as he brings his fingers to his mouth, sucking off my pleasure.

Hot as fuck.

I'm in so much trouble. He smirks at me and leans in to whisper, "So sweet. Told you I could have you singing in under three minutes. Just so you know, I'm going to need more. When the lights go out again, it's time for dessert."

He takes my hand and leads me back to our table. I take a much-needed drink of wine, but I think I need water to cool me off after all that. The next singer takes the stage, and I try to focus on her but I feel Jimmy watching me. Finally, I turn to look at him and he's smiling his most mischievous smile.

"Do you feel proud of yourself?"

"Actually, yeah. You know why? Because now when you hear Kostas, you won't think about how hot he is, but how hot *I* make *you*."

I roll my eyes and throw my hands up as I laugh. "You're such an arrogant ass! Is that the only reason why you did that?"

"No. That was just a perk." He shrugs and then leans forward on his elbows. "I did it because I got so fucking hard watching you dance. Once I got my hands on you, I had to be inside of you. I didn't have enough time to whip my dick out so...I went with," he wiggles his fingers at me like he's casting a magic spell. I don't know whether I want to laugh or throw a basket at his head.

The music changes again, but this time it's very upbeat. It's a mix of belly dancing, but with a pop beat. I give him a naughty smile and stand. I deliberately perk out my ass and breasts as I make my way to the steps of the stage. Other women have already come up here to dance, so I ease my way into the group but remain easily visible to Jimmy's hungry eyes. If my last little dance did something for him, wait until he sees what I have in store for him this time. *Let's see how far I can push his limits.*

As I close my eyes and feel the music, though, I forget about trying to drive Jimmy wild. I get lost in the hypnotic melody and the freeing feeling of just letting my body flow to the rhythm. I feel the velvety soft texture of flower petals slide down my skin. I hear the sound of hands clapping close to me and feel the warmth of his body before I see him. I know before I open my eyes that it's Jimmy behind me. I smile up at him, and in a sultry voice, speak with a Greek accent, "Dimitri."

"Koritsi mou." His Greek accent, combined with that husky voice, sends a shiver down my spine. "You put on quite a show."

"Glad you decided to join me."

"And miss out on dancing with the most beautiful woman here? I'd never forgive myself. And I don't believe in living with regrets, koritsi."

The music changes as a male singer walks out on the stage. The clarinet and bouzouki are in full swing for this one. I notice more men come to the stage as some people form circles. I remember this from that night at the house, so I begin clapping and kneel in front of Jimmy. I reach over and tap the person next to me. I point to Jimmy and make a show of kneeling and clapping. They get my drift and join me in kneeling and clapping. Jimmy bites his bottom lip as he shakes his head at me. The person next to me yells something in Greek, but I assume it's for him to come on and dance. Jimmy nods and begins dancing. Other people join our little group and cheer him on. I can't help but notice women undressing him with their eyes. He's like a feast for them. What they see is a gorgeous man who's confident enough to dance in front of everyone—and his confidence is sexy as hell. What they don't see is his good heart, passion, sense of humor, and ... that I'm falling completely in love with him. *No, no, no.* This is for fun. I shake my head and clap to the beat. Jimmy smiles at me, and it's so infectious that my smiles spreads wider.

When the song ends, everyone claps and pats Jimmy on the back. Before we make our way off stage, I wrap my arms around him and kiss him. He may not be mine forever, but he sure as hell is tonight. As we pull away, flower petals rain down on us. I laugh and look over to see Kostas. He grins and begins singing to us. He bends down and picks up more petals off the stage and tosses them on us. He stands between me and Jimmy as he continues to sing. Then, I hear a second male voice, and Kostas stops singing to cheer. "OPA!"

Kostas steps back and hands Jimmy the microphone. Jimmy takes it and keeps his eyes glued on mine as he sings with the band. Who knew he could sing? This arrogant, sexy Greek bastard can do everything.

I wish I knew what words he was singing, but the way he smiles at me and his eyes burn, I have an idea. He pours so much passion into the words as he takes

ARROGANT ARRIVAL

my hand and places it on his chest above his heart. He holds it there as his hips gently sway to the beat. When the chorus ends, he hands the microphone back to Kostas to finish the song.

When we get to our table, I pull Jimmy in for a hug. "That was so amazing. I've never been serenaded before."

"Me neither." Jimmy smirks.

"Shut up. I mean it. That was so romantic, even if you were probably doing it just to be a ham and show off yet another amazing talent you have."

"Another amazing talent? How about I show you the one talent I'm most proud of?"

"What's that?"

"I said let me show you..." Jimmy raises his eyebrows and leads me to a dark corner. He sits me on a stone ledge.

"How'd you know this was here? Have you done this before?" I look around making sure that we're completely hidden. I can still hear the loud music and cheering.

"I've been scoping the place out." He slides my panties down and then shoves them in his pants pocket. "Sshhh. You don't want us to get caught..." He spreads my legs and then smirks at me, "...or do you." Before I can answer, my words get stuck in my throat.

And he's taking me to heaven all over again.

Jimmy

It's four in the morning by the time we make it back to our room. Despite having no sleep, I have to have Jolene. I've teased and tasted her all through the night, and now I plan to feel every inch of her body with mine. As soon as the door shuts to our hotel room, I grab her face and crash my lips to her. I lead us to the bed without breaking contact with her lips. We pull and tug on our clothing to quickly get them removed. There's no foreplay because that's been happening the entire night. I pound into her, and she loves it, and I don't stop until I've given her every last drop of me. Then, we both crash.

I don't even remember falling asleep. I wake up to the sound of my alarm. I'm also naked and half on top of an equally naked Jolene.

"Did we pass out after having sex?" I grumble as I try to shut off my phone alarm.

"I guess I was just that good." She responds with her eyes still shut. "You're welcome," she yawns.

Jolene rubs her eyes and groans. "Fuck. We've got to get going. We have to be at the port in an hour." She turns on her side and throws her leg and arm over me. "I don't want to leave."

"I don't want to, either." What I don't say to her is... *I don't want this to end.*

CHAPTER 21

Jolene

Jimmy and I stand at the front of the ferry as we pull away from the island. I feel like a part of my heart has been left there. The ferry boat cuts through the sparkling clear blue water as the island becomes smaller, almost like it was just a fantasy. I already long to have back my mornings of sleeping in naked and wrapped between sheets and Jimmy, eating delicious food from fresh ingredients from a grandmother's recipes, and watching the sunset on the beach before dancing the night away into the early morning. The unanswered question hangs heavy between us. We only have two days left, and then the vacation is officially over—*this between us* is over. We go back to our *separate* lives in America.

The wind whips my hair around. Jimmy nudges me. "You're being quiet."

"It's windy. You wouldn't be able to hear me, anyway, between the wind, waves, and ship's engines."

"Let's go inside then."

"No. I want to look at the island for as long as I can."

"Why?"

"To make sure it was real." *That this between us was all real.*

We each carry our luggage to the front of the condo. Before Jimmy opens the door, he turns to me and says, "You're almost free. Think you can keep putting up with me for two more days."

I have no idea how to take that. Is he joking because he's happy this is almost over, or is he trying to hide his disappoint as much as me? "Two-and-a-half days, actually. This day is almost over."

"Don't resort to counting down the minutes or anything," he mumbles as he opens the door.

Martha, who must've heard the door, or better yet, was probably watching the window, rushes into the living room to greet us. "Did you have a nice time?"

"It was so beautiful. I got to use some of my dance moves I learned from here the other night."

"Oh, you went dancing! How wonderful. I hope you did better there than you did here." *Ouch.* I thought I was an amazing dancer that night. She smiles and then turns to Jimmy. "You got some color to your cheeks. If you get any more, people will think you're a gypsy."

His grandmother comes in and scoffs. Jimmy laughs at what she says in Greek and turns to me. "Yia-Yia says I already am a nomad. I can't stand to stay in one place too long."

ARROGANT ARRIVAL

"That's true. A pilot with his wings. You're like a bird flying around, landing where the urge strikes you."

Jimmy turns to his grandmother and I assume he translates what I said because she looks to me and nods. She says something back to him and his mother. Whatever it is, they both look at me with wide eyes full of alarm. Then, with a smug smile, the little old lady shuffles to the other room.

Martha mumbles something about preparing dinner and leaves the room. I tilt my head and ask, "What did your yia-yia say?"

"Um, she said eventually birds make nests and something about plucking off wings. I don't even want to think about what she meant by that."

"Worried something—or someone—is going to pluck your wing?"

"You better watch it before I pluck you."

"Hey, guys!"

I about jump out of my skin when I hear Bianca behind us. I turn around and smile. "Hey! Did we miss anything?"

She smiles as Georgina tugs on her hair. "Not much. We spent most of the days on the beach drinking coffee and eating."

I think about it and then smile. "Same here."

"Well, I guess we're getting the full Greek culture then," Bianca laughs. "If you're tired of spending all your time with that knucklehead, want to join me and Georgina on the beach? Dex has a phone conference, so he is going to be holed up in the room for a minute."

"I'd love to! Let me go put my bag in my room and put on a swimsuit." I join Bianca and little Georgina on the beach. We swim and play with pebbles. After a while, I insist Bianca allow me to hold Georgina so she can stretch and relax.

"Jolene?"

"Yes?"

"I think it's real for him."

My heart stops. "What is?"

Bianca scoffs and I can practically hear her rolling her eyes. "Don't even. I don't think Jimmy is completely faking this. Maybe at first...but I don't think he wanted to let you go earlier. The way he's looking at you. Something has shifted."

"I don't know about that."

"He's a decent guy. He can be a little bit of a pain, but deep down, he's a really good guy. Please don't hurt him."

"Bianca, I–"

"I know it's not my place."

"It's just that it's easy to get lost here. Reality doesn't exist anymore it seems. Especially when you're in paradise. Everything is so beautiful and vibrant. When we get back home and to our real jobs...I think then we'll see what was real and what was fantasy."

Bianca goes quiet, so I focus back on playing with Georgina. She tries to stick a pebble in her mouth and I try to distract her by tossing the pebbles at the waves as they come to the shore. Bianca surprises me when she whispers just loud enough for me to barely hear.

"What if the fantasy was never a fantasy to begin with...but instead it was all reality?"

I ignore her comment and close my eyes, letting the sun warm my skin. Something hard hits my knee

ARROGANT ARRIVAL

and I'm startled awake. A gorgeous man stands before me. The sun is shining bright behind him, making him literally glow, and having me wonder if this is a dream.

"Sorry, miss. Are you hurt?" *Whew. That accent.*

I blink a couple of times to clear my vision. He's tall, muscular, with a little dark hair on his chest, black wavy damp hair, and a face beautiful enough to make angels weep. He picks up a volleyball and then extends a hand to me. That must've been what hit my knee. I stand up and then accept his hand.

"I'm Marco."

I smile and continue shaking his hand. "I'm Jolene."

"Ay! You are American?"

"Yes."

"I'm from Italy. I'm here with my brother and cousin on vacation."

"Same." Then I shake my head. "Not with my brother or cousin, but I'm here on vacation."

He chuckles and looks down at our still-joined hands. "Would you like to play ball with us? I could use a partner."

I turn to Bianca who's biting back a smile. She nods her head and shoos me with her hand. I turn to Marco with a shrug. "Sure."

I walk a few feet away from Bianca and wave to the brother and cousin. Wow. What a family. All three men are gorgeous and fit. I've only gotten a few spikes in when two strong arms wrap around me from behind, causing me to yelp.

Marco frowns at me and those playful brown eyes turn hard. I can hear the smile in Jimmy's voice as he says, "There's the love of my life."

"The love of your life? Really, Jimmy."

He chuckles in my ear. "Just letting these Italian bitches know they're playing with what's mine."

"What's yours?"

"This trip isn't over yet, koritsi mou. You're all mine, *still*."

Deciding to mess with him, I pull from his arms so I can face him. I smirk and side-eye the Italian men. "Those Italians, though. Whew. Maybe I want to play with them?"

Jimmy frowns and pulls me to his side. He starts stomping through the sand with me firmly against him as he grumbles, "Yeah, well, you're stuck playing with a second-rate Greek."

Jimmy

"She doesn't want a relationship with me. She'll want to go back to having nothing to do with me once we leave here. We leave Greece, we leave the fantasy," I tell Dex. We met up in the kitchen, both hungry after he finished a business call and I finished some calls for flights booked next week.

"So? Bianca was skeptical about me at first too. She called me *Mr. Moneybags*. You didn't lie to her about what you do, did you? Because I can tell you from firsthand experience that *that* does not end well. It did end well, actually, for me, but I wouldn't recommend it."

"No. I did at first—well, I didn't lie. I just didn't tell her, but then she found out and that turned into her storming away. But fate has brought us back together. I know it. I can feel it. I just don't know if she can see it."

Dex pops a grape in his mouth and chews. After he swallows, he says, "Be honest. You have to be honest with her and yourself. Just tell her how you feel. Tell her you want a relationship with her and see where it goes from there."

I pull a few grapes from the bowl and pop them in my mouth. Between chews I say, "Yeah, okay. But she didn't even want a fake relationship with me, so I seriously doubt her wanting a real one with a pilot, no less."

"Exactly. No woman wants a *fake* relationship. Show her that you're offering her something real, pilot or not."

And with those words of wisdom, he walks out the door.

CHAPTER 22

Jolene

Dear Journal,

Tomorrow we leave. Tomorrow this all ends. Will Jimmy and I keep in touch? Could we possibly even have a relationship? I get upset over people letting me down, but I've let myself down. I promised myself I wouldn't fall for another cocky pilot—yet here I am. Maybe it's just being in Greece. Maybe when I leave paradise, the magic surrounding us will clear and so will these silly ideas in my head. That's it. It's just because we're in Greece and pretending to be in love. We can't possibly be in love. I barely know him. This isn't a love story, or one of those silly love songs. This is real life. Our whole relationship started with a lie, and it will end with a lie. I've fallen in love with a lie.

ARROGANT ARRIVAL

I go into the kitchen and find his mother and his grandmother working on preparing dinner.

"Can I help?" I hate how small my voice sounds, but I already know I'm not their favorite. I just really need something to do.

They both look at each other, and then Patty gives me a curt nod. Wordlessly, she hands me a long, thick cucumber and mumbles something in Greek. I look between the two ladies, and Martha says, "She's not speaking about you in Greek to be sneaky. She doesn't know English. But yes, she is talking about you. She said you probably know how to handle something like that." Martha goes back to stirring whatever she has in the pot. Then, she looks back to me. "And she didn't mean cooking."

"Thanks. I got that." Inhaling a deep breath, I pick up the cucumber. I smile at Patty and shake the cucumber while nodding. "Yes. Me know." Then I take a knife and chop the tip off. I smile back at her with my maimed cucumber. Yia-Yia bursts out laughing and pats me on the back. Just like that, we go to work on supper in comfortable silence.

After dinner I sit out on my room balcony and watch the waves coming in. I still can't believe some people get this view every day. I sit on my balcony back home and all I see is another concrete building. That thought depresses me.

"Hey, you." I look over and Bianca has walked out to her balcony. "I was thinking. Maybe you could write something like a blog post and I could send it to my boss? Write about your trip here."

"I don't know—"

"You have time right now, and besides, look at your inspiration." She points to the ocean. "Don't settle, Jolene. If you don't want to, fine, but if you're wanting to do something else, now's the time to do it."

"It's that easy, huh?"

"It's that easy."

"Shouldn't I be packing? We leave tomorrow."

"In Greece, the night is young." She goes back to her room and I hear her balcony door sliding closed.

Of all the phrases she could've used. *The night is young.* I grab my phone and swipe the screen. I decide I'll just play around with what I would say *if* I did write a silly travel piece. *Greece offers the best beaches. Greece offers amazing cuisine from family recipes passed down for generations. Greece offers...* I look down to see Jimmy walking shirtless on the beach. *Romance.*

Instead of focusing on writing a good travel blog piece, I write something for me. My fingers can't move fast enough as the words pour out of me. Greece offers everything a tourist could dream of, but it also offers more than that. It offered me an opportunity to find happiness and a chance of tasting not only the most amazing cuisine, but also love.

Before I can even read over it again or think better of it, I send an email to the address Bianca gave me. I refuse to even look back over what I'd written. The words were raw and probably revealed more than what I'd like to show. Either way, it was nice getting them out.

ARROGANT ARRIVAL

I look back down at the beach, but Jimmy's not there any longer. My heart deflates a little until there's a knock at my door and now my heart is in my throat. I turn around, and there's Jimmy. My emotions are still too raw from what I'd written. I really don't need to see him right now. But he doesn't wait for an invitation. The door clicks when he shuts it, and then I hear the lock click into place. I stand and come inside from the balcony. I slide the door shut and also lock it. We meet each other in front of the bed. Jimmy begins unbuttoning my shirt. His blue-green eyes swirl with a cloud of emotion, but he doesn't speak. He doesn't have to. I can read all the same frustrations and uncertainties in his eyes that he can probably see in mine. This is our goodbye. Maybe it doesn't have to be, but neither one of us is going to cave, that much is evident. So, we'll let our bodies do the communicating.

I shiver as my shirt falls to the floor, and Jimmy's warm lips touch my collarbone. I reach behind and unfasten my bra. It slides down my arms and joins my shirt on the floor. As Jimmy's lips make their way down to my breasts, I unhook my khaki shorts. Then I unhook his. I sit on the bed and scoot toward the top. Jimmy crawls up after me like an animal in search of its prey. I'm all too eager to become his evening meal.

What starts out as slow sensual touches and kisses, soon turns into hunger and passion. His hands grip each part of me tightly as if I'll disappear if he lets go. My hands greedily grab him everywhere and pull him closer. Even though our bodies are flushed together, I need him closer and deeper. Our movements are jerky, as if we can't get enough and we know we're running out of time. Each kiss and touch are precious moments we won't get back, and yet we both want it all. All at once. I want him everywhere, except for the one place where he already is—my heart. He's there but I'm not sure I can handle him leaving without a backwards glance.

Despite the bed squeaking and the headboard hitting the wall, I hear a rumble. Then glass crashing downstairs. I look up and the clock on the wall is shaking.

"Jimmy," I pant. "I think there's another earthquake."

"That's just me, baby, rocking your world."

He would think that.

Downstairs, someone calls up, "Earthquake."

Jimmy looks at me, "Should we stop and go downstairs?"

I'm so close...and this feels sooo good. If I have to die, this is as good a way to go as any. Jimmy keeps moving in and out of me, and I moan. His movements turn slower and harder. "Well? Want me to stop and we go outside?"

There's another rattle but it's smaller. "It's just a little one, right?"

Jimmy frowns and goes in deeper. "What's a little one?"

"Jimmy? Seriously? I think you're insecure. Don't be so defensive. I meant the earthquake."

"Let's see who can do more shaking." And with that, he goes all in.

ARROGANT ARRIVAL

Jimmy

Jolene insists on getting dressed before we go downstairs. She said she is not going to let everyone see her naked *again*. So the earthquake is over by the time we...and, well, she got dressed. Dex comes walking over to us outside. "Did you guys feel the earthquake?"

"That was just us. Sorry about the scare, everybody. Ow!" Jolene smacks the shit out of my chest. I lean into her ear and whisper, "Sweetheart, that shit is fine in the bedroom, but not otherwise. I only enjoy my pain as long as it's accompanied by pleasure."

She smacks the shit out of me again as everyone laughs.

We go back inside and hang out in the living room. Dex and Bianca bring Georgina over. They sit cuddled together on the couch while Jolene and I play with Georgina on the floor. I make one of her little stuffed puppies bark and Jolene takes another stuffed puppy and has it pretending to lick Georgina's face. Both of their sweet giggles melt my heart. I feel as though I'm being watched, and turn to find Yia-Yia's appraising eyes. She's almost blind, but she doesn't miss anything. Sensing the wheels turning in her head, I stand and go sit next to her.

In Greek I ask her, "What is it?"

"You should marry the American."

"What?"

"Marry that girl."

"Wait, we'll swing back around to that. You knew she wasn't Greek?"

"Dimitrios, you are such a bright boy. Where do you think that came from? Your mother and father? No. You get it from me. I'm not stupid. The first time that girl ever even tasted anything Greek was when you stuck your tongue down her throat."

"*Yia-Yia.*"

She shrugs as though to say *it's true*. "Marry her."

"Why?"

"Because she is the one for you. She would not clip your wings, but instead fly with you. When you two are together, your love soars. That's happiness, Dimitri mou. My dying wish is for you to find someone with your spirit and love. Birds do build nests, Dimitri mou, but they still fly."

"Are you saying we're birds of a feather, Yia-Yia?"

"What I'm saying is don't let her fly away from you. Let her fly *with* you."

I swallow the lump in my throat at her words. They ring more true than she knows, or maybe she does know. Little old Greek ladies have some mystical powers. That's why everything that they cook tastes better.

Jolene stands and smiles. "I think I'm going to take one more stroll down the beach. I'm going to miss... all of it." She hurries out and I watch after her. I turn to Yia-Yia who raises a single white eyebrow at me. I scowl and then hurry after Jolene.

"Wait up. I'll join you." I fall into step next to her.

"What did your grandma have to say? You looked pretty tense."

ARROGANT ARRIVAL

"That I'm a bird."

"Ha. Again?"

"Yup. She also told me I'm thoroughly flocked."

"I doubt she said that."

"She did... in so many words."

She laughs and the sound physically hurts because I want to hear it every day, but I'm too much of a damn coward to tell her. Multiple times on this trip we teased each other about being a chicken and the reality is that it's me. I'm the chicken. *I really am a fucking bird.*

We begin walking back toward the condo. "I'm thinking about applying for that job with Bianca's magazine. She said I could work from anywhere, so that'd be nice."

"That would be."

"I may or may not keep my current job if I get it. I'll for sure cut back on my hours."

"That would be a good idea. Probably. If that's *truly* what you want."

We approach the back door. I watch her inhale and then exhale as she waits for me to say something. I don't know what she wants me to say. She can make any career move she wants. She doesn't need my approval. With a sigh, she turns and goes into the house without another word.

I think I just flocked up.

I stand at the beach a little while longer. I need to figure out what the fuck I want. I think I want Jolene. She's perfect for me. She doesn't take my shit and keeps life interesting. We both have careers that would allow us to live anywhere. This was a trial relationship run, in a way, and I don't want it to end. I think I want the full subscription. She doesn't seem like she wants it to end. We should make it permanent! *Why am I still standing here with my toes in the sand?*

I hurry back to the condo. I rush through the door, past Ma and Yia-Yia. I take the stairs two at a time. "Jolene!" I open her bedroom door, but it's empty. "Jolene?"

"In here," a voice purrs. Looking over my shoulder at my cracked bedroom door, I narrow my eyes. The room is dark, but that's where the voice came from. I hesitantly open the door the rest of the way. "Jolene?"

A throaty chuckle greets me as I enter the dark room. "No, someone better."

My balcony door is open, and lying on my bed basked in moonlight is Pamela wearing only red lingerie. Her lips are painted in red and she's wearing red heels. Yet nothing about me craves her. I don't find anything about this sexy or hot.

"Yeah, I don't see better. Maybe it's the wrong lighting for you, sweetheart."

"Oh, Dimitrios, you've always had such a mouth on you. Why don't you come show me if your mouth can do anything other than spew lies and sarcastic comments?"

"I'd hate to disappoint you. Get dressed and out of my room."

"Jimmy!" *Oh, God, no!* My eyes widen in panic when I hear Jolene's voice. "Jimmy, did you call out my name?"

ARROGANT ARRIVAL

"Get. Out." I ground my teeth at Pamela. I do *not* need this shit right now.

"Sure." Pamela smiles. She slides off the bed and walks toward me.

"What the fuck! What are you doing?"

"YES! Yes, Jimmy. Mmmmm."

I try to get away from Pamela as she kneels in front of me with her hands gripping my belt. Jolene walks in and gasps. My hands are gripping Pamela's shoulders as she kneels before me.

Jolene's bottom lip trembles. "I guess I imagined hearing my name."

Pamela licks the corner of her mouth and smiles. "You've imagined a lot this week."

I shove Pamela away and turn to Jolene, but she holds up a hand. "Don't. Don't let me interrupt." She takes a step forward but then stops. Turning back around, she smiles. "Actually, you know what? I think I will interrupt. You interrupted my plans for me to come here with you, so allow me to inconvenience you for five minutes." She charges over and points a finger at Pamela. "I hope you know this doesn't mean you've won. It just shows that you really are a universal whore. Congratulations."

Jolene rears her arm back, and then sends her fist into Pamela's nose, knocking her on her ass with a cry of pain. Pamela holds her nose as she tries to stand. I don't see her leave the room because Jolene's eyes are bright as she turns them on me. "Malaka!"

Even though I know the hit is coming, and I brace for impact, I'm so surprised by the force behind her punch...so much so that I stumble backwards. I grab my jaw and stare wide-eyed at Jolene. Her face wears a strong mask, but her eyes are bleeding before me. She turns back around walks away.

I want to scream for her to listen to me. Let me explain. But what can I say? Pamela set this up to where there's no way Jolene would believe me. My mind races with what I should do, but I finally get my dumbass in gear and rush after Jolene. No matter how much I cry out her name, she doesn't slow down. She runs out the door. Before I make it to the door, Ma stands in front of me.

"Jimmy mou! What's happened?"

"Did you know? Did you help arrange this?"

"What are you talking about? Why would I ask what happened if I knew?"

"Then who let Pamela into my bedroom?"

Ma gasps. "Your *bedroom?* She came over, asked about you, and then after a cup of coffee said she needed to go to the restroom. Then you walked in and ran upstairs. I figured she hadn't come back because you bumped into her."

"Yeah, you could say I bumped into her. She was laid out half naked on my bed, and practically assaulted me. Jolene walked in and..."

"Oh, Jimmy mou. No adrouli mou." She takes me in her arms and hugs me. "She'll come back. Let her cool down, son."

Yia-Yia clears her throat. "Don't be a fool. Go after her. At least let her know you're not still in the bedroom."

I run out the door and go next door to Bianca's condo. She answers but hasn't seen Jolene. I jog into

ARROGANT ARRIVAL

town. Running down each street, quickly scanning everywhere for her. I stop and place my hands on my knees. My lungs are burning and my heart feels like it's about to pop out of my chest. I didn't know a broken heart could still beat, but it does. I search all night, but there's no sign of Jolene.

CHAPTER 23

Jolene

"I basically wrote it out for him. I'm willing to try new experiences and I'm going to be working with his cousin's magazine. You know what his response was? *Nothing.* Instead, I go back to the house and find that Greek whore on her *knees* in front of him." I hiss into my cellphone. I've just arrived at Athens International Airport. I'm about to tell the family goodbye, and then head back to my life. *Alone.*

"What did he have to say? Did you knock her on her ass?" Lana asks.

"You bet I did," I huff out. "I didn't need him to explain. It was pretty clear."

"Why?"

"If he wanted a relationship with me, then he would say so. He would ask me to be with him. He would fight for me. Instead, he went and got a sendoff and showed me just how ready he is to commit."

Lana loudly sighs into the phone. "Really? I don't know, it sounds like you two were heading somewhere."

ARROGANT ARRIVAL

"We were until we came to a fork in the road apparently."

"Are you not a strong independent woman capable of thinking for herself? What's with you? In every area of life, you go for what you want except for intimacy. You'll ask a man to sleep with you but not *be* with you? Plus, you told him you don't date pilots, so maybe he's scared he'll get rejected again."

"I'm just tired of having to beg–"

"Spare me the bullshit. I think you need time to figure out what you want and then go after it. Whether it's a relationship or new career. Nobody needs to give it to you, and nobody needs to approve of it. You decide what you want and then go after it."

"Go after it."

"Yes, go after it. But don't think anyone rejected you until they actually have said those words. Don't let that bitch take what you want. You do have a mouth that you can use for something other than–" I end the call before she can finish that sentence.

Turning on my heels, I head back to the group. Since I didn't want to see Jim again, I stayed with Bianca and Dex last night. I hated asking Bianca to lie to her cousin for me, but she did when he came by. I've taken a flight leg to work to get back home earlier than planned, for obvious reasons. They leave Greece today as well, and Dex offered to drive me. It was a sweet offer, but it's time for the lies to end and for me to travel solo again.

"My cab should arrive at any moment," I smile and say to Dex.

"Well, I guess we better get this over with before your cab arrives. Don't want to miss your flight," Dex says as he extends his hand to me.

The door opens and Martha and Patty hurry in. I stand tall despite my nerves. What if they reject me and don't even bother saying goodbye? Should I go ahead and save myself by waving bye and running off?

Bianca turns to me and I take little Georgina's hand in mine. "I'm going to miss you, princess."

"You don't have to. You can visit any time. Besides, I'll be in touch about the blog."

Unsure what to say to that, I give her a small smile. Jim's mother and grandmother stand before me. "It was wonderful meeting you both, Martha and Patty."

Patty shakes her head and points to herself. "Yia-Yia." She takes my hand in both of hers and squeezes it. "Kortisi mou." She pulls me down and takes my cheek in her hand as she kisses one side, and then the other. She points to herself again. "Yia-Yia," she says as she begins to shuffle toward the door.

I want to cry. She asked me to call her grandmother. I didn't even think she really liked me. Martha's eyes are glassy as she lifts her hands but then drops them. Then, she lifts her hands again but hesitates. Finally, she comes up to me and wraps me in a hug. "You are, in fact, a good girl. I know what I said to you earlier. All I'm saying now is please don't break his heart."

I wrap my arms around her and gently squeeze. In her ear I whisper, "What if he already broke mine?"

In a deadly calm voice, Martha's Greek accent rings clear. "Then we clip more than his wings."

ARROGANT ARRIVAL

We both laugh as we pull apart. The door bursts open, and Jim runs in with red-rimmed eyes surrounded by dark circles. Martha pats my cheek and turns to Jimmy. "Adrouli mou, I'll give you two a moment. I'm going to take Yia-Yia and get a coffee, 'kay?"

"Yeah, Ma. Will you get me something, too?"

She nods and waves bye to me, leaving me alone with her son. Jimmy takes a few steps closer to me. "I guess you're free of me?"

I nod. "I guess you're able to spread your wings now and fly off. Free as a bird."

"Listen, whatever you think...I'm sorry. Nothing happened."

"If nothing happened, then why are you sorry?"

"Because, either way you got hurt, and I was the cause of it, *again*."

A car honks outside. Not being able to stand the awkward tension building around us anymore, I decide to take my leave. "Goodbye, Jim."

He reaches out to me, but I jerk out of the way. I hurry to the door and take off toward the cab before the tears start falling. I quickly get in and ask the driver to leave. I don't look back.

At the airport, I get in the line for airline employees and pray everyone will move faster. Once I'm through, I faintly hear what sounds like Jim's voice calling out to me.

"Jolene! Jolene! Wait!"

My phone buzzes and I see it's him calling me. But I'm a coward...I keep walking, and I don't look back. I hurry to my flight where the crew is already waiting.

Unfortunately, of all the pilots to work this flight, it's Trip. Renee walks up looking fabulous while I feel like I'm on the verge of tears.

"So what happened with your Greek god of the sky?"

"I thought I was God of the sky?" Trip jokes.

"Jo, here, was with her very own Greek demigod." Renee jokes.

"Wait...the contract pilot? You stayed in Greece with him? Didn't he have a family?"

I want to groan. Trip already didn't think very highly of me, and now he thinks I'd go as low as sleeping with a man who has a family. Just because I hit on him while he was with Kendall does not mean I lack every moral fiber. In my defense, they weren't *together*. Standing tall, I try to maintain what dignity I have left, "He was with his family, but it wasn't *his* family. He was with his mom, cousins, his niece, and... Yia-Yia." I smile.

Trip beams and his eyes brighten. "That's really nice, Jo. Greece, huh? That must've been amazing. He seemed like a nice guy."

"He was."

"Was?"

"Nothing came of it."

"Now, Jo. Don't waste time wondering. I know that look. Kendall and I missed out on so much time that we could've been making memories together. Everything worked out in the end, but it still pisses me off. *Wasted*. Lost time that we won't get back...and for what?"

I look around and Trip notices my unease. He takes my arm and leads me over to a more private area.

ARROGANT ARRIVAL

"Listen to me, Jo. Call Kendall and ask her. Maybe a woman-to-woman convo might help. We've known each other a long time. I don't want to see you make the same mistake I did. Call him. If you like him and think you two had a connection, chase it down. I had to. And I could kick my own ass that it took me so long before I did. Do you have his number?"

"Yeah. He tried to call me, but I was...this is so embarrassing. He tried to reach out to me once we left each other just now but I was too scared. I wouldn't answer his call. I'm afraid he is going to love me and use me, and I like him too much. I wouldn't survive the fall for him."

"Are you kidding me? You can't be serious, Jo." Trip shakes his head. "I know we didn't work out, but I was an asshole. And maybe this guy is an asshole, or maybe he used to be. It sounds like the guy is trying. Now, it's your turn to try."

I feel my eyes begin to water and a short laugh escapes me. "I didn't expect you to be the one to give me relationship advice."

Trip wraps his strong arms around me and laughs. "Hey, Jo, remember to let him into your heart, then you can start...to make it better."

"Wow. That's nice, Trip."

"The Beatles were very wise. Now sounds like you have found your Mr. Right, now go and get him."

I laugh, "What?"

Trip smiles. "My spin on 'Hey Jude', from..."

I smile, "The Beatles."

Once all the passengers are settled on the plane, I put in a single ear pod. Kostas Dalaras' soothing voice begins singing. I don't know what he's singing about, but the melancholy melody fits my mood. Maybe it's about a time when the nights were young? Maybe it's about a love left in paradise? I don't understand the words, but I definitely understand the ache in his voice.

One week later...

I decide that I need time to figure out myself. I know what my heart wants, but I'm still a mess. First, I call the airline and let them know I want to cut back my hours. If I get hired with the magazine Bianca works for, maybe I can even afford to quit completely. I spend my entire day off working on a personal travel blog. Even if nobody reads it, it's therapeutic to write about my journeys and feelings. Plus, now I'll always be able to look back and recall these memories.

I've just finished getting my website how I like it when my cell rings. *Bianca.* I swipe the screen and answer.

"Hello?"

"Hey, I have some news!"

Is it Jimmy? Does he miss me? Is he wanting to meet? "Oh, yeah? Well, what is it?"

"They loved your piece! They want an interview. Are you available this week?"

"Yes! Oh my gosh, yes!"

I'm so excited. Someone read my words, and they loved it. What now? Can I do it again, or was that just a fluke? Either way, I can't wait to move forward. I spin around and do a little happy dance. I'm beyond ecstatic for this next journey of my life, but my heart is still missing a piece of it. I want to know about Jimmy. I wait, hoping she'll volunteer the information, but instead she keeps talking about the job—which is important too. Finally, I can't take it any longer and ask, "Any other news?"

"Nope. That's it. I look forward to seeing you next week!"

And with that, she hangs up and I'm left hanging. I should've swallowed my pride and simply asked what I wanted to know. Why didn't I? Now I'm going through the whole day wondering and missing him because I'm a fool. I'm about to go to sleep when my phone dings with a message from Lana.

> Lana: Thought you should see this.
> Lana: ATTACHED VIDEO

I click the link and it sends me to YouTube. The screen is black, but then the words flash across: *To anyone who is lonesome because they lost their sweetheart. This is for you, koritsi mou.* The screen fades and there's Jimmy sitting in a chair in the back of a plane.

"I just landed but didn't feel like going home and being alone. I keep thinking about this girl. This incredible woman. I wonder what she's doing and if she's thinking about me. So, I found this song fitting. Since I'm sure she's blocked my number, I'll post it here and see if fate can intervene and send her my message."

He strums the guitar and then begins singing, "Are You Lonesome Tonight." I listen to it. And then I listen to it again. And again.

I wake up around six in the morning determined to get myself where I want to be. Despite not going to sleep until about two because I was listening to Jimmy sing on repeat, I'm full of energy. I open my journal from my past trips and begin typing away several articles for the magazine. Around one in the afternoon, I realize I haven't eaten. A peanut butter sandwich will have to do because I'm on fire. If I leave the house, I might lose my mojo. Quickly, I take a bite out of my sandwich as I carry it to my laptop. Between bites and chews, my peanut butter fingers fly over the keys. *I'll worry about the mess later.* The words are pouring out of me now, there's no slowing down and no stopping. This feels right. This feels like something I've been missing in my life. I love traveling, and now I can share my adventures. There's something therapeutic about reliving these experiences and putting the words out there. It's even better than when I write in my journal. The magazine might not even publish these on their website, that's a hard and definite possibility. I won't know until I try, but right now, even trying is helping me find a piece of myself, so either way, this is an accomplishment.

CHAPTER 24

Jimmy – One month later...

"**D**id you read it?"

My milkshake and burger arrive. I smile at the waitress and thank her before answering Bianca on the phone. "Read what?"

"The article I sent you."

I place my phone down and put it on speaker. Then I go to my email. My heart stops in my throat when I see who the author is.

In Greece, the Night is Young by Jolene Tanner.

"What about it?" My voice is tight as I close my eyes shut. "I guess she got the job. That's great."

"Just read it. I know you miss her."

"Sure. Anything else?"

"No. Have a nice flight. Thank you for delivering the plane."

I end the call and debate if I want to even read the article. This woman destroyed my heart. Do I have the courage to read her words? I take a bite out of my cheeseburger and swipe my phone screen. I sip my chocolate milkshake as I read about *our* trip together. I slam my phone down because I don't understand. She writes as though she fell in love with me, but maybe that's just to sell magazines or encourage people to book travel arrangements and get people to travel to Greece.

"Will passenger Jim Georgakopolous please come to the service desk?"

I listen again. "Will passenger Jim Georgakopolous please come to the service desk?"

I pay my bill and go to the service desk. I wait in line, and then my eyes widen and see why I was paged overhead when I see her. Jolene appears and waves. "Hi, Jimmy."

"What are you doing here?"

"Waiting for you to arrive."

"You paged me?" She nods. "Why? How'd you know I'd be here?"

"Bianca told me. By the way, I've missed you."

I shake my head. "I called you for two weeks straight. You couldn't answer your phone? Not *once*. Respond to my messages? You ignored me after everything we shared. And now you show up and tell me you miss me?"

She hurries toward me, but I step back. I'm wounded and angry. She doesn't get to ignore me and then suddenly decide she's ready to pick up where we left off. I shake my head and turn to leave. She calls out to me, but I give her the same courtesy she did me...I keep walking.

The overhead speakers in the sound system crack. Then, it's not English but Greek. A woman is singing...

ARROGANT ARRIVAL

that can't be. I turn around and stare. Jolene holds the receiver to her mouth as she sings *in Greek* the Kostas Dalaras song I sang to her. I shake my head in wonder and walk toward her. She stops and walks around the counter to me.

"When did you learn that?"

"I kept listening to it after I came back. After a few times, I was able to sing along, although I have no idea what I'm saying."

I swallow the lump in my throat and shake my head. "What changed, Jo? Why now? Why did you run off like that and then fall off the grid?"

"I was hurting."

"And you think I wasn't? I still am! Jolene, nothing happened. Pamela set that whole thing up. I was trying to get her to leave when you walked in."

"Your mother called me. She told me."

"You'd listen to her, but not me? After everything?"

"I knew before she called that you didn't do anything. But I needed some time to work on me, Jimmy."

"Maybe I still need some time."

"Jimmy, I realized that while we were in Greece, that was the only time I ever slowed down. It was the only time I ever enjoyed life. Also, I wanted to make sure you weren't just a fling for me."

I take a step back. Wow. Twist the knife a little more in my heart. It hurts that she couldn't tell the difference between what we shared and a fling. "Either you care for me, or you don't. Either you want a relationship, or you don't."

I turn around, but stop when I hear, "*Wise men say...*"

I turn around to see Jolene holding the intercom and singing one of Elvis's greatest hits, "Can't Help Falling in Love."

I watch as her skin begins to turn a nice shade of pink. Slowly, I walk toward her. Her eyes never waver from mine. When I'm standing toe to toe with her, she whispers, "Falling in love, with... you."

"I've never been serenaded before."

"I have. Only once. Thought I'd try it out."

"Oh, yeah?"

"Yeah. Did it work?"

"No." She dips her chin, and I lift it up with my two fingers. "I was already in love before you even began."

She wraps her arms around me, and people clap as her lips meet mine. Tired of our relationship always being a show for bystanders, I lead her away. "So you write a travel blog now?"

"Yeah, if only I had a pilot to assist me with it because I have a lot of places I need to visit."

"Stop. You're just doing all this to get access to my cockpit."

"Is it working? At least the cock part?"

"You know there's no issues with that part working."

"I love you, Jimmy."

I stare wide-eyed at her. "Come again?"

"I love you."

I search her eyes and can't stop the goofy smile stretching across my face. "I love you, koritsi mou. Let me see if I can get my flight canceled because I think I've arrived at my final destination."

"Oh, yeah? I think our adventures are just getting started, pilot."

ARROGANT ARRIVAL

"What about for tonight?"

Jolene surprises me further when she says, "I nychta einai nea, agape mou."

The night is young, my love.

EPILOGUE

Jolene – One year later...

It's been a year, and I'm back on the same bridge in Greece eating ice cream. I now work full-time writing travel blogs and columns. Jimmy is still a contract pilot. Best of all, we work together traveling the world. Each day we share is a new adventure. And I think that on each adventure, I fall a little more in love with him. He's still an arrogant Greek ass, but that's part of his charm. He's fully committed to loving me, and making me feel loved. His family wasn't shocked that I'm not really Jolene Tannerelos. I think Jimmy is the only one that really thought that scheme would work. When I told him as much he replied, "But it did work. I've got you, don't I? So it worked well enough for me."

Jimmy takes my hand and leads me to the center of the bridge. I hear the faint sound of the bouzouki. The music grows louder, and I realize it's coming from a boat that's floating toward us. I am almost positive they're playing an Elvis song.

ARROGANT ARRIVAL

I cross my arms. "What are you up to, Jimmy mou?"

When I turn toward him, Jimmy gets down on one knee. He takes my hand with his fake engagement ring that I still wear. He slides the ring off and then reaches in his pocket. He holds a replica of the ring and smiles. "Jolene Tanner, will you be my real fiancée?"

My ice cream cone falls out of my hand as I cover my mouth. Tears build in my eyes. This time, I don't even hesitate. "Yes."

Jimmy's smile shines brighter than the sapphire in the ring he slides on my finger. On closer examination I see that this ring has a rose gold vine, and tiny diamonds accent the sapphire. He kisses my finger wearing the ring and smiles at me. "I got you a real ring this time."

"It's perfect."

"What would you like to do now, koritsi mou?"

"Everything! The night is young, agape mou."

The night is young, my love.

**Want to keep up with all of the new releases
in Vi Keeland and Penelope Ward's
Cocky Hero Club world?
Make sure you sign up for the
official Cocky Hero Club newsletter
for all the latest on our upcoming books:**

https://www.subscribepage.com/CockyHeroClub

**Check out other books
in the Cocky Hero Club series:**
http://www.cockyheroclub.com

ACKNOWLEDGEMENTS

What an honor to be a part of the Cocky Hero Club! I can not thank Vi Keeland and Penelope Ward enough for taking a chance on me. This is an amazing opportunity, and I hope my story did justice to their world. Thank you so much!

And the simple fact, that you the reader took time out of your life to read this story makes my heart feel like it's about to burst. I love you! Thank you!!

Thank you so much to every single reader, blogger, and fellow author that has taken a chance on me. I've made some wonderful friends along this journey. I appreciate and love you all so much.

I have to thank Gail's Book Belles. My wonderful reader group. You people are the main ones that keep me going. Your posts and comments make my day. Love you!

Amber Hall – Jimmy's Elvis obsession was for you! I hope you like the songs and enjoyed that little tidbit about him.

My mom. She has an incredible talent for finding humor in every situation. People that have met her, they always comment on how she's always laughing and smiling. The woman has a witty comeback, pun, or joke for *any* given moment. I'll always appreciate that about her, along with her love for reading. Granted –

this isn't a typical book my mom would read. I love you more!

The Hrissikos and Panousis family – they exposed me to the amazing Greek culture and welcomed me into the family. Note – none of my characters are based on the family.

George and Emily – for answering all my questions about the world of pilots and flight attendants. Yes – I exaggerated some of the situations. Another side note – none of the characters are based off real people or events.

Thank you to my amazing group of friends and support team!! Thank you for always checking on me and keeping me sane! I value your honest feedback and input so much. You all definitely make up a huge part of Gail Haris. I love you ladies and appreciate our friendships!!

Author Jessy Lin – I have to give you a special shout-out because let's be honest, I wouldn't have pushed forward without you. THANK YOU! You believe in me, even when I don't. We're doing this together!

My big sister, Teresa. I wouldn't even be an author if not for you. I didn't know the indie book world existed until you encouraged me to read on e-reader. You instantly encouraged me to write my own book. There's a reason I went with 'Gail.' We both share that name, and I'm so grateful I'm sharing this journey with you. There's no way any of this would've happened without you. I love you, sis!

Elaine York – my amazing editor! Thank you for continuing to encourage me and believe in my stories!

I love working with you! More than that, I'm so grateful for the friendship we've formed. Thank you!

Nicole Thompson – What was Kiki thinking by introducing us?! Trouble in the making ;) I'm so thrilled our paths crossed. Thank you for supporting me and becoming my right hand gal! I swear, I feel like we were the guys from Step Brothers – and instantly became best friends. You don't watch movies but just go with it.

Kiki Chatfield – I met you at a book convention and knew instantly, I wanted to work with you. Your spunk, drive, and passion for books is inspiring. Your guidance has helped me grow so much. More than anything, you're an amazing friend to have in my corner.

Next Step Pr Team – Epic. That is all. I love y'all!
My husband.
My freaking, incredible Greek husband.

You support and believe in me means more to me than you'll ever know. Thank you for tolerating me on days I'm stressing out to meet a deadline. You work tirelessly to support our family and, on top of that, you've helped with our girls so I can pursue my dream.

To my girls. My beautiful and intelligent girls. I thank God every day for blessing me with you two. You both are the reason I strive to be a better person. You're the reason behind my decision to go after my dream. My dream now is that you both achieve your dreams.
If I've failed to mention anyone, I'm truly sorry. I love you all and I'm so grateful for all the support. Thank you!

ABOUT THE AUTHOR

Gail Haris believes in fairytales, love, and laughter as the best medicine.

She was born and raised in a small town in the Southeast Missouri. After graduating with a degree in Mass Communications, Gail went on adventures traveling in America and Europe. Her favorite adventures are still the ones when she gets lost in with a book.

Her love for reading and traveling lead her to attend book conventions. Those conventions gave her the encouragement she needed to combine her passion for creativity and storytelling. Using coffee and her imagination, she loves writing contemporary romances that blend laughter and true love out of everyday chaos.

When Gail isn't day dreaming in front of her computer, she's busy raising her two daughters with her best friend and biggest supporter – her husband. She loves traveling with her family and friends, binge watching television series, singing Disney songs with her daughters, and having huge family and friends get-togethers that involve lots of food and usually a cake.

She hopes by following her own dream of becoming an author, she can set an example to her daughters that dreams can become reality. Maybe she can encourage you too.

Never stop believing in love, dreams, and yourself. And coffee...don't give up on coffee and books ;)

CONTACT GAIL

gailharisauthor@gmail.com

https://gailharis.com/

FACEBOOK PAGE:
www.facebook.com/pg/authorgailharis

FACEBOOK GROUP:
www.facebook.com/groups/gailsbookbelles

INSTAGRAM:
https://www.instagram.com/authorgailharis/

TWITTER:
https://twitter.com/GailHaris

GOODREADS:
www.goodreads.com/author/show/19815494.Gail_Haris

BOOKBUB:
://www.bookbub.com/authors/gail-haris

NEWSLETTER:
https://mailchi.mp/c741d7956650/ghauthor

COLISEUM
ROMA
NEW YORK CITY
MONUMENT VALLEY
GREECE